Vincent Eyre

Lays of a Knight - Errant in Many Lands

Vincent Eyre

Lays of a Knight - Errant in Many Lands

ISBN/EAN: 9783337292133

Printed in Europe, USA, Canada, Australia, Japan

Cover: Foto ©Andreas Hilbeck / pixelio.de

More available books at **www.hansebooks.com**

LAYS OF A KNIGHT-ERRANT IN MANY LANDS.

BY

SIR VINCENT EYRE, K.C.S.I. & C.B.

MAJOR-GENERAL, ROYAL ARTILLERY (RETIRED).

LONDON: HENRY S. KING & Co.

65 CORNHILL AND 12 PATERNOSTER ROW

1874

To

C. M. E.

the constant companion of my wanderings in many lands,

THIS VOLUME

of wayside warblings and random rhymes

is

𝔇𝔢𝔡𝔦𝔠𝔞𝔱𝔢𝔡,

as a Christmas "Souvenir,"

by her

loving and loyal

"KNIGHT-ERRANT,"

V. E.

PREFACE.

THIS volume is intended solely for the entertainment of innocent and juvenile minds irrespective of age.

Three months of almost continuous downpour of rain during the autumn of 1872 in our northern counties, drove the writer to the south of Europe in search of the truant sun; but, failing to find that lost luminary even in that comparatively favoured region, he embarked for Egypt, and there beheld the object of desire waiting to greet him with even too warm a welcome.

After a pleasant sojourn of three weeks in Cairo, a party was formed for ascending the Nile as far as Philæ. The boat—one of the largest on the river—was christened the "*Star of India.*" We constituted the magic number " Seven," and called ourselves " THE PLEIADES."   Five were ladies. For mutual edification we agreed to keep a " Log-book," wherein each was to scribble whatever and whenever the spirit moved.

The writer's own share of these contributions constitutes PART I. of this volume.   Ordinary prose seemed too tame a vehicle of expression for the thoughts and feelings inspired by the scenes we were daily witnessing ; hence these impromptu and unstudied effusions in rhyme, which helped to en-liven our small party on board, and may perchance answer a like purpose with others similarly situated.

PARTS II. AND III. comprise, with a few excep-tions, scraps of verse dashed off at random on all sorts of occasions for the amusement of friends, young and old.

PART IV. is the result of sharing a German governess with a young lady during some other-wise dull winter days at Vevey. The subjects were derived chiefly from the poetical part of " Otto's Grammar," and have been included in this collection only in deference to the opinion of some competent German scholars, who consider they successfully embody the style and spirit of the originals. The only excuse to be offered for such a medley of trivialities is that well-known line in Virgil,

"Cantantes licet usque, minus via lædet, eamus."

Or,

"'*Tis lawful as we toil o'er life's highway,*
To cheer the journey with a tuneful lay."

V. E.

ATHENÆUM CLUB, *Dec.* 1, 1873.

CONTENTS.

PART I.

Contents. xi

PART IV.

LIST OF ILLUSTRATIONS.

PART I.

LAYS OF PHARAOH-LAND.

LAYS OF A KNIGHT-ERRANT.

A New-Year's Day on the Nile.

1

IN joyous sunshine, fanned by balmy breeze,
On Nile's broad stream we hail the bright New
    Year,
On ottoman reclining, stretched at ease,
Beneath the awning of our duhabeea ;
With outspread sail our southern course we steer,
Leaving the storms of Europe far behind ;
Yet mindful still of absent friends most dear,
Oh! where else, if not here, shall we contentment
    find ?

2

As dream-like, noiselessly we glide along,
In moving panorama we survey

Scenes that to earth's old history belong—
Tombs of the mighty dead long passed away,
And Pyramids still struggling 'gainst decay;
Recalling many a scene of Bible-story,
When Pharaoh's host marched forth in strong
     array,
Defiant of Jehovah's might and glory,
And were o'erwhelmed with fate retributive and
     gory.

3

At Cairo we first boarded our small ark,
United in one laudable intent—
To leave behind all thoughts morose and dark,
And gratify our own peculiar bent;
Meaning thereby each day should be well spent
In study and fine arts from morn till even,
Flavoured with words and deeds benevolent:
We form, in fact, the magic number "SEVEN;"
The same as those sweet stars, the "PLEIADES," in
     heaven!

4

The "Star of India" is the outward sign
And symbol of our floating habitation,

Like that of Bethlehem, whose ray benign
Betokened "peace and good-will" to each nation;
May such prove our own final destination!
And though our ladies are as *five to two*,
May they spare us poor men all botheration,
Acting, as all good angels ought to do,
To their liege loving lords aye generous and true!

A Startling Incident.

—o—

A STARTLING incident occurred : we passed
A duhabeea with disabled mast ;
Upon its deck two graceful females stood,
Waving their handkerchiefs in frantic mood ;
Beside them were their husbands, friends, or
    masters :
Can they have wanted aid for their disasters ?
The "Stars and Stripes" were fluttering from the
    stern ;
The name, with aid of glass, we could discern—
'Twas the *Sultana ;* and it roused our pity
To think that *one* at least was young and pretty !
What should we do ? "Ho ! dragoman, dost hear ?
Forthwith to yonder boat we wish to steer !"
The callous wretch looked at us with a snigger,
And seemed as hard to move as any nigger.

Quoth he, "They're merely *waving a salute ;*
To stop in such a breeze would never suit ;
Moreover, there's a steamer in the rear
Can tow them on, if they feel any fear."
While arguing thus, we onward fast had sailed,
And thus our chivalrous intentions failed :
I feel quite sore about that sweet young woman,
And fear she'll harbour doubts if I'm a true man !

Excursion to the Caves of Beni-Hassan.

—o—

[These caves contain the oldest known paintings in the world,
illustrative of the daily life of the ancient Egyptians before
the time of Moses.   The name of King Osirtasen the First,
who reigned B.C. 2020, occurs among the hieroglyphics over an
entrance.   He ruled over the whole country from the Delta to
the Second Cataract.]

Lo ! Beni-Hassan's wondrous caves
Enticed our party o'er the waves ;
Leaving our *Star* with flying pennant
In the safe charge of our lieutenant,
Across the wide Nile we were rowed,
With lots of grub in basket stowed ;
Over the sands and fields we wended,
Then up a rugged steep ascended,
Which led us straightway to the spot
In front of a sepulchral grot,

Whose entrance porch afforded shade
Beneath which our repast was made;
For Britons, go where'er they will,
Are in hot haste to take their fill.
This being done, we felt at ease
To roam about where each might please;
So now within the Caves we entered,
And on their walls our gaze was centered;
For each upon its surface bore
A library of painted lore,
Where we the social life might scan
Of this old world's primæval man;
And truly glad we were to find
He wore *no monkey's tail behind !*
In fact, he seemed almost to be
Of our sweet selves *facsimile.*
Like us, they ate and drank and fought,
And fish out of the river caught;
They hunted game, caressed their wives,
And led most fashionable lives;
For though their worship was a riddle,
Right well they danced to fife and fiddle;
And though the ladies wore no stays,
Their slender waists deserve our praise;

Nor deem me daft if I declare
That *some wore chignons in their hair!*
In fact, they seem, in form and features,
To have been darling little creatures.
Having at all the pictures looked,
King Osirtasen's name I booked,
Much to a Yankee friend's amazement,
Who wondered what my eager gaze meant,
And doubtless deemed it quite horrific
To waste my time on hieroglyphic.
In the big boulders scattered round
All sorts of fossil shells we found,
Proving the ground whereon we stood
Had once been covered o'er with flood,
Long, long ago, when men were varmin,
According to the book of Darwin,
Though for my part I'm satisfied
To have come out of Adam's side.
Having enjoyed our day's diversion,
Thus ended our first land excursion.

Excursion to the Town and Caves of Sioot.

—o—

[SIOOT is the capital of Upper Egypt, and is the site of the ancient
LYCOPOLIS, or "City of Wolves," which animals were worshipped there and embalmed. The face of an adjacent hill is
perforated with numerous mummy-caves of very ancient date.]

SIOOT is reached—the old "Lycopolis"—
Of Upper Egypt the metropolis ;
We land amid a crowd of donkeys,
And boys, all chattering like monkeys ;
We mount—each little quadruped
Has saddle-cloth of dazzling red ;
We number four—away we start,
And onward to the city dart.
Like chessmen of gigantic size,
Its tall white minarets arise
Above a crowd of flat-roofed houses,
Where dwell the "Fellahs" with their spouses.

We enter a long covered street,
Where some queer spectacles we meet :
Women and men in strange attire ;
Moslems with scowling eyes of fire ;
Nubians whose wide mouths grin at us
Like those of hippopotamus ;
On either side an open shop,
Whose owner calls on us to stop—
Nor calls in vain.   We buy some ware,
Of curious shape and fashion rare :
One lady (men's belief 'twill stagger)
Invests some money in a dagger ;
So, lest some mischief she might mean,
I take its fellow, just as keen ;
But hope the day may never dawn
That sees us two at *daggers drawn !*
At length we reach the Post-bureau,
And in the box our letters throw ;
Thence, passing to the outward plain,
A view of some high cliffs we gain,
With mummy-caves all perforated,
As we had found by " Murray " stated.
At the hill's base some tombs are clustered,
Where many modern dead are mustered ;

Whence upwards our procession wends,
And each from donkey's back descends.·
Above us, soon an ancient cave
Invites to contemplation grave :
At the door stands a figure tall,
Carved in the rock ; within, a hall
Vast in dimensions ; each wall covered
With signs not easily discovered.
Beyond, enveloped all in gloom,
We pass into another room,
And, with the aid of some wax-tapers,
Trace some quaint figures cutting capers,
Or doing " heav'n knows what " !   The ground
Is strewed with old bones all around ;
Men, wolves, and monkeys in confusion,
And in most horrible profusion.
After this anatomic glut
Once more into the air we strut,
And there see, prodigally spread,
The beauties of old Nile's broad bed ;
A thousand fields of shining green ;
Above, a sky of blue serene ;
A breeze whose every breath is bliss ;
Oh ! what is pleasure, if not this ?

Enough—'tis time to end our ramble,
So downward to the boat we scramble ;
Once more remount each scarlet saddle,
And homeward to our boat skedaddle.

Excursion to Abydus.

—o—

[The ruined temples of SETHOS and RAMESES II. at Abydus are
among the chief attractions of the Nile. They date from the fourteenth century B.C., which appears to have been the "Augustan
age" of Egypt; during which art and architecture attained
their highest development. In each of these temples a tablet
was placed, whereon was recorded a complete list of the seventy-
six kings, from MENES downwards. That of SETHOS is quite
perfect, and supplements what is wanting in the broken tablet
of RAMESES in the British Museum.]

1

HELP! Muse of Egypt! if there be
Any such kind divinity;
   Oh! aid my verse!
Our ride on asses from ABYDUS,
Preceded by a man to guide us,
   I'll now rehearse.

2

Our route lay o'er twelve miles of ground,
Our beasts no bigger than a hound;

There was a lack
Of ordinary riding-gear,
And we felt puzzled how to steer
Thus far and back.

3

But, after an hour's hideous row,
We managed to get off somehow,
And half-way stopt
Beneath a roadside mansion's shade,
Where coffee for us all was made
By a kind COPT.

4

A misadventure here occurred,
Somewhat unpleasant, though absurd :
A saddle shifted
Whereon a dame sat posed in state ;
And round she twisted on her pate,
Her heels up-lifted !

5

Ah ! 'twas a sight to rouse the pity
Of gods and men, that one so pretty
Should thus be humbled ;

Swift to the rescue we all rushed,
To save her head from being crushed,
    Or bonnet tumbled !

6

Though stunned, there was no need of plaster,
And, rallying soon from the disaster,
    She bore her part
In friendly converse with the Copt,
And a large slice, I fear, she lopt
    From off his heart !

7

Resuming our adventurous way,
'Neath the full force of solar ray,
    O'er boundless fields
We saw arrayed in greenest dress
What stores of wealth, man's toil to bless,
    Kind Nature yields.

8

We reached at noon the desert range
Of rock and sand that mark the change
    From life to death ;
Where desolation's lot is cast,
And relics of long ages past
    Lie hid beneath.

9

Here, lost to modern sage inquiries,
Lies buried deep the great *Osiris*,
        Enwrapt in mystery ;
The object once of adoration
To the old, old Egyptian nation
        From dawn of history.

10

Here, SETHOS, ere his rule was done,
And RAMESES, his warrior son,
        Raised each a fane
Whose wondrous ruins still attest
The skill by architects possessed
        Throughout their reign.

11

Into the former as we entered,
Our gaze upon a group was centered
        Of German gobblers,
Who, in the very holiest part,
Were feasting on meat-chops and tart
        Like famished cobblers.

12

Great SETHOS ! how thine injured ghost
Would have rejoiced their limbs to roast

O'er hottest fires!
Thus to defile those sacred halls
Recording on their storied walls
Thy kingly sires!

13

From MENES, founder of thy race,
Each regal name thou here didst place,
That future ages
Might render tribute to their glory,
And make immortal Egypt's story
In history's pages.

14

And though thy race be passed away
Amid long ages of decay,
Still be thy deed
Held by all noble souls in honour,
Though mourning Egypt wears upon her
The widow's weed:

15

Though her great day of might be gone,
And her degenerate sons now groan
'Neath tyrant's sway,

Still let the memory of the past
Over her present darkness cast
        Its deathless ray !

16

Having thus moralised awhile,
We sought out a secluded aisle
        For our own dinner ;
For PHARAOH'S self, were he our judge,
Would not some crumbs of comfort grudge
        To a poor sinner !

17

To Nature having tribute paid,
Back to our boats all haste we made,
        Halting awhile
At the Copt's hospitable gate—
Right glad to sleep, though somewhat late,
        On dear old Nile !

The Temple of Denderah.

(*The Ancient Tentyra.*)

———o———

[This is one of the most perfect of old Egyptian temples, and was in course of erection when Christ lived at Jerusalem in the reign of Ptolemy XI. It was dedicated to ATHOR, the Goddess of Love and Beauty, before whom the sculptures, which cover the walls, represent the kings of Egypt with propitiatory offerings in their hands; and among them is the celebrated Queen Cleopatra.]

I

BEHOLD another wonder of the Nile !
   Another glimpse into the misty past !
Within TENTYRA'S desolated pile
   We roved 'mid sculptured walls and columns
      vast,
Where none dared enter once save king or .
      priest ;
But now, profaned by tread of man and beast,

2

Here ATHOR, Beauty's goddess, was adored
 By rulers of mankind, who offerings brought
Of earth's best produce, lavishly outpoured,
 And for their reigns her stanch protection
  sought;
Nor, judging by her smile benevolent,
On stone recorded, was she malcontent.

3

For then, as now, 'tis plain that Beauty's power
 Was paramount in all affairs of men;
And still, to her, ev'n kings their standard
  lower;
 Nor need she care for gorgeous temples, when
In every heart of man she finds a throne
Where she may reign unrivalled and alone!

4

Nor all in vain did Egypt's beauteous queen
 At ATHOR'S altar pious vows fulfil;—
Her triumph came, when at her feet was seen
 The CÆSAR, captive to her charms; and still
The name of CLEOPATRA lives to grace
The memory of her vanished dwelling-place.

5

Thus, not without some sympathy of soul,
   We viewed this tribute of old heathen kings
To one o'er whom e'en Death hath no control ;—
   That mystic power whose praise each poet
     sings ;—
All else may fade, but LOVE shall perish never :
Is it not writ, " *Your heart shall live for ever ?* " *

* Ps. xxii. 26.

A Misadventure.

A PROVERB says, " *The more haste the less speed !* "
Just now it hits us very hard indeed ;
Ladies somehow are always in a hurry,
And thereby oft occasion needless worry ;
So ours must needs insist that, without fail,
The *Rais* should at all hazard carry sail,
Even should in the *night* a breeze arise ;
And lo ! it comes ! our bark before it flies ;
'Tis early morn, but darkness broods around,
When suddenly, *bump, bump,* we are aground !
Oh ! impotent result, fraught with disaster,
Of feminine impatience to go faster !—
On a stiff sandbank hard and fast we stick !
" Off to the village ! summon hither quick
At least one hundred ' fellahs' to our aid ! "
Promptly the sapient order is obeyed ;

But soon 'tis found much "easier said than done,"
For fast as men are caught away they run ;
Though, after much delay and trouble plenty,
A gang is brought to bear, who muster twenty ;
But all in vain ! they push and pull and yell,
Not all their efforts make us budge one ell !
And we seem doomed our voyage here to end
Unless kind fate should some assistance lend ;
When, lo ! a timely steamer from the rear
Arrives, and promptly dissipates our fear ;
Consents from off the bank our bark to tow ;
Hurrah ! we 're free once more, and off we go !

Thebes.

—o—

[THEBES extends over many square miles on both banks of the
Nile, very much as Paris and London over those of the Seine
and Thames.   On the east bank are the temples of *Luxor* and
Karnac ; on the west, the temples of *Koorneh, Dayr-el-baharee,
Dayr-el-medineh, the Ramesium, the two Colossi,* and *the Valleys
of the Kings and Queens,* containing the cave-tombs of ancient
royalty.   The existing monuments belong chiefly to the thir-
teenth, fourteenth, fifteenth, and sixteenth centuries B.C.]

O THEBES ! thy wonders 'mid remotest ages
Formed a fit theme for ancient bards and sages ;
But how shall my poor unskilled modern muse
Presume to thrust my toes into their shoes,
Or strive in lofty lay with them to vie,
Without their wings through fancy's realms to fly ?
Still, since our Log demands renewed attention,
I must proceed our recent deeds to mention ;
Behold us, then, at THEBES, where MENES reigned
Sometime before the flood ; 'tis not explained
How he and his escaped from being drowned,
And thus contrived a dynasty to found ;

But we are bound to take facts as we find them,
And these old kings have left such marks behind
    them
As to this day the minds of men astonish,
And modern feeble vanity admonish ;
For Pharaoh's royal race reigned here, and
    flourished,
Ere infant Greece had yet been born or nourished,
And ere the father of the Jewish race
In Egypt sought out an abiding place,
When his fair SARAH was in no small danger
Of being taken from him by a stranger ;
For Pharaoh, thinking she was ABRAM'S sister,
Found she had raised within his heart a blister ;
Which might have led to some domestic strife
Between the faithful Patriarch and his wife !
At all events, we can't such proof refuse
That Pharaohs flourished long before the Jews.
Here, then, with certainty we look around
And know we really tread on ancient ground,
The very cradle of our human history,
Though shrouded still by a thick veil of mystery ;
And, much as we lament that superstition
Should have debased, thus early, man's condition,

We still must feel no little admiration
For what remains of this primæval nation,
Who have bequeathed such vestiges gigantic
In the stone records of their deeds romantic ;
Showing how RAMESES with spear and bow
And his sole arm slew thousands of the foe,
Bearing off captive scores of foreign kings
To his great temple's god as offerings ;
How SHESAK led proud JUDAH'S king in chains,
And spread alarm o'er PALESTINA'S plains ;
How OSIRTASEN spread Egyptian sway
From Ethiopia's wilds to ocean's spray,
To where Nile's waters with the salt sea blend,
And, in their fertile course, vast fields befriend.
Here THOTHMES, too, has left whereby to trace
One of the mightiest of a mighty race ;
His obelisk* at ROME points to the skies,
And tells us of this world's changed destinies.
Nor be forgotten SETHI'S pictured tomb,†
No longer walled up in perpetual gloom,

---

* The obelisk of the Lateran at Rome bears the name of THOTHMES III., who reigned about 1463 B.C.

† This is the magnificent tomb discovered by Belzoni fifty years ago. Its bas-reliefs and paintings represent the various stages of the soul after death until its final admission to eternal happiness.

Where still OSIRIS to men's fears appeals,
And the dread secrets of the dead reveals.
But, lo ! what GIANT IMAGES are those
Seated amid the fields in stern repose ?
Like petrified survivors of the race
Who raised the massive structures of the
    place,
They gaze in scorn at man's degenerate state,
And morbidly lament old Egypt's fate.
"Ye pigmies of the earth ! " they seem to say,
"Why toil ye thus in vain from day to day ?
Like ants ye labour and like vermin die,
Leaving no trace, like US, of *majesty !* "
Thus MEMNON mocks, though "vocal" now no
    more,
Each passing traveller rushing the world o'er,
Ever in search of some new strange excitement :
Say, doth not wisdom echo the indictment ?
As for ourselves, we took it not to heart,
Though we might feel a momentary smart,
And, in revenge, we sketched each ugly feature
Of those two monster forms of human creature ;
And having curiosity indulged,
We pocketed the insult thus divulged.

My guide was a bewitching little creature,
Of gender feminine and pleasing feature :
Two smaller nymphs my roving footsteps followed,
Like "Graces" the "Apollo;" though they holloaed
Somewhat too oft for " *Bukshcish ;* " still, I felt
Proud of my trio, and benevolent ;
For " FATIMA " was musical in speech,
And eager to learn all that I would teach ;
Nor, truth to say, did she display much greed,
But showed herself a maid of gentle breed,
Helping me much to buy old curiosities
In shape of beetles, mummies, and monstrosities :
I gave her of my love a token plain
Which meant *" Dear girl, we part to meet again ! "*
A *pair of scissors*, to assuage her pain.
Farewell to THEBES ! a tempting northern breeze
Urges us onward ; thus the more one sees
The more the passion grows. So now our plan
Is to push on as far as ASSOU-AN.

" *El-humda-lillah !* "

(" *God be Praised !* ")

—o—

[A triumphant Ode in celebration of our arrival at the First
Cataract.]

I

" *El-humda-lillah !* "   Thus to heaven
  In joyous burst of praise
Let the full choir of " Pleiads " * seven
  Their grateful voices raise ;
Conducted safe from courtly Cairo
To this far boundary of Pharaoh ;
Where many an overhanging pile
Of granite rock hems in the Nile,
    Man's enterprise oft checking,
    And his frail vessels wrecking ;

---

* The number of our company being *seven*, we called ourselves
the " PLEIADES."

While monster boulder-stones of size gigantic,
Heaped up together in confusion frantic
      On every mountain top,
      Seem ready down to drop ;
As though the fragments of some ruined world
Had by contending fiends been at each other hurled:

2

" *El-humda-lillah !* "   Have we not,
   With favouring northern breeze,
Visited many a famous spot
   In luxury and ease ?
Viewing, in one long panorama,
Scenes of the old world's wondrous drama ?
Temples and tombs and mummy-caves,
Along the course of Nile's wide waves,
      In form and size stupendous,
      And of an age tremendous?
And have we not, too, seen huge crocodiles,
And pelicans by hundreds on small isles ;
      And groves of feathery palms,
      And sunset's glowing charms,
Each day supplying some new pleasant theme,
Till all around seemed one long and delightful
      dream ?

3

" El-humda-lillah 1 "   Can we e'er forget
   Those happy tranquil days?
While poor old England has been drenched with
      wet,
   We 've revelled in warm rays
Of glorious sunshine, amid scenes of beauty,
Far from the fogs of regions dark and sooty ;
No bitter mingled with our sweet,
Save that time sped along too fleet !
    Ah ! oft when all seems drear,
    May these bright memories cheer
Each drooping heart amid life's dull decline,
And, like the sunset's glow, around us shine !
    And may the friendly union
    Of our Nile-boat communion
Be lasting as the " Pleiades " above ;
That, though we met as strangers, we may part in
      love !

A Souvenir of Philæ.

[The island of PHILÆ, situated above the First Cataract, is perhaps
the most attractive spot on the Nile. The temples date from
the time of the early Ptolemies at the beginning of the Christian
era, and seem to have been dedicated chiefly to the worship
of Isis, Osiris, and Athor (goddess of love).]

OUR southward pilgrimage at PHILÆ ended,
That frontier of the Pharaohs, whither wended
In ancient times the devotees of ISIS,
Who came to seek indulgence for their vices,
Or take a peep at ATHOR'S lovely face,
Which there in her own temple found a place.
OSIRIS also was supposed to sleep
In some spot hereabouts, in cavern deep ;
Though, as his body was hacked all to bits,
And scattered among various mummy pits,
It seems most probable, upon the whole,
That what thus "slept at Philæ "* was his *soul.*

---

* Herodotus always alludes to Osiris as "*he who sleeps at Philæ.*"

But be that as it may, this much is clear,
He had two lovely goddesses quite near
To guard his slumber, causing him to keep
Always one eye wide open in his sleep !
Volatile British females ! look around !
The isle whereon you tread is holy ground ;
Perchance OSIRIS still with flail might thrash
Sinners like you, should you deserve the lash.

.   .   .   .

Beautiful PHILÆ ! fitly chosen spot
For gods and goddesses to fix their lot ;
Here NILE, imprisoned 'mid huge piles of rock,
Bursts through his bonds with swift impetuous
      shock,
Yet lingers lovingly with outstretched arms
To fold in fond embrace thy tempting charms ;
Jealous to leave thee in grim Vulcan's lap,
Too fair a nymph to waste on such a chap !
Still may be seen the impress of his lips *
Ere downward on his headlong course he dips.

---

* The allusion here is to the deep grooves in the rocks, worn by
the strong current of the Nile during countless ages.

Pilgrims of love, we felt its potent power
While musing 'mid those scenes in eve's still
          hour;
What wondrous tales might Philæ's piles unfold,
Of many a maiden fair and warrior bold,
Who came from far their simple vows to offer,
And drop their pious gift in priestly coffer!
Since then, what scores of centuries have sped!
Worshipped and worshippers alike are fled;
Vast ruins cover the once sacred ground,
And silent desolation reigns around;
Whilst, to record his own and country's shame,
Each modern idiot carves his worthless name,
 Nor spares the very features of the gods.
Rouse up, OSIRIS! ply thy vengeful rods!

                .   .   .

PHILÆ! farewell!   'Mid life's distracting duties
Oft shall the vision of thy varied beauties,
Like a bright dream, the saddened soul beguile,
While fancy floats us once more on the Nile,
And sees the feathery palms their foliage wave,
And the wild rocks watch round OSIRIS' grave,

Like fossil giants of some Pharaoh's reign,
Waiting in hope to see him rise again.*
Thus far to sunny South, in wake of swallow,
We 've fled from cold, but can no farther follow ;
Now to our native North we turn again
With patriot's pleasure, not unmixed with pain ;
For life, alas ! is like Nile's flowing river,
And downward as we float, the more we shiver,
Sharing reluctantly its ceaseless motion,
That mingles us at last with dark oblivion's ocean !

---

* The Egyptians believed in the future resurrection of OSIRIS to judge the world. He was put to death by TYPHON, the incarnation of evil, and his body cut into fragments, which were collected by ISIS and buried in various places, of which *Philæ* and *Abydus* were the most sacred. OSIRIS is always represented with a *flail* for the punishment of the wicked, and a shepherd's crook for the guidance of the good.

Down the Nile.

—*o*—

1

RIGHT-ABOUT-FACE !—Sweet sunny South, good-
    bye !
  Northward we turn our melancholy gaze ;
The rising Pole-star fronts us in the sky,
    Rearward the " Southern Cross " melts in the
      haze ;
Down Nile's mysterious stream we slowly glide,
Whose secret source let LIVINGSTONE decide.

2

But oft our boat, like a young bashful girl,
  Seemed half afraid to face the rude north wind,
And curiously from side to side would twirl,
  As if it really knew not its own mind.
'Twas torture thus to crawl in crablike fashion,
But 'twas no use to get into a passion.

3

Our crew's proceedings were a constant puzzle,
  Spasmodically fast and slow by fits ;
Ofttimes in full career they 'd stop to guzzle,
  While our good *Rais* seemed to have lost his wits
Ever since parting from his Nubian spouse
At ASSOUAN, where he possessed a house.

4

Of course we stopped at EDFOO'S stately pile,
  Sacred to HOR-HAT, ATHOR, and young HORUS;
And viewed the temple of the Crocodile
  At ancient OMBOS, with no boys to bore us :*
At SILSILIS those quarries we surveyed
From which so many structures vast were made.

5

We also landed oft to grope about
  In sundry grottoes smelling strong of bats ;
But all the mummies had been taken out
  Of men and crocodiles and birds and cats,
And other creatures scarcely worth the cost
Of thus embalming, since 'twas labour lost.

---

* The village-boys of Egypt seem to consider it their special
duty and privilege to worry travellers, and may be fairly classed
with *flies* in the category of modern Egyptian plagues.

6

One morning, mightily to our amaze,
  A boat in full sail hailed us as she passed,
And suddenly, to our astonished gaze,
  A bag of English letters to us cast;
Some newspapers were also with them hurled,
Giving us the last news of all the world;—

7

Foremost and first,—the poor French Emperor
    dead!
  By German bullets spared to die in peace,
Far from his subjects, in an English bed;
  Gone to that world where earthly troubles cease;
Once fickle Fortune's favourite, at last
A vanquished fugitive;—now all is past!

8

Thus has man's mad ambition been reproved
  Since history's dawn;—witness these scenes
    around,
Where mighty kings majestically moved
  Like gods, and worshippers by millions found.
Where are they now?—their tombs and temples
    where?
Naught—naught is left but desolation bare!

9

Once more at THEBES !—We took a moonlight
    stroll
  Amid the gloom of KARNAK'S columned
    halls—
Rich treat for an imaginative soul,
  Provided that no ghostly fear appals,
And donkey-boys can be bribed into quiet;
I recommend all travellers to try it.

10

The valley of the "Tombs of ancient Kings"
  Afforded a fine field for exploration;
Of their contents each learned guide-book sings,
  And every fool records his name and nation,
Knowing right well he has no other hope
Whereby from dull obscurity to grope.

11

With rapture I renewed my fond alliance
  With gentle Fatima, my donkey-lass,
Who quite returned my flame, and frowned defi-
    ance
  On jealous rivals; so it came to pass

That she and little Miriam took their seat
Near me when tired, and *tickled both my feet.**

12

And I commend this pleasant operation
 To every weary traveller on the Nile,
Recording here my self-congratulation,
 However envious critics may revile.
Ah! if I could but have my wicked way,
Those girls my feet should tickle every day !

13

Well, the sad moment came at last to part
 From the nymph FATIMA, and THEBES, and
I hope for a small corner in her heart, [LUXOR ;
 Even should she become some Arab's " *uxor !* "
Our next adventure in our Nile-life's lottery
Found us at KENEH, famous for its pottery.

14

The British Consul there, of visage black,
 Seemed to appreciate a fairer skin ;
He came to dine, and made a brisk attack
 On potent wine, which raised such fire within,

---

* The intention was to *shampoo*, but the sole result of their in-
fantine efforts was that above stated.

That he insisted we should forthwith go
To see some dancing-girls he had to show.

15

In short, he got obstreperous, and swore
    He would not budge an inch till we agreed.
With one consent we voted him a bore,
    Of whom it much behoved us to be freed ;
So briefly he got hint 'twas time to go ;
And off he went—" sad, melancholy, slow ! "

16

How shall I utter what I saw one morn ?—
    A holy saint of fourscore years and ten,
Sinless and robeless as a babe just born,
    Seated upon a bank since deuce knows when.
Over the elements he holds dominion,
'Tis said—but that is matter of opinion.

17

As " SHAIKH SALEEM " he is known in these parts,
    And navigators hold him much in fear ;
Because, unless appeased, a curse he darts
    Whereby boats oft are lost in their career ;
Though, for my part, I think a wholesome *washing*
Might be well supplemented with a *thrashing*.

18

But now my muse your charity beseeches ;
    A vile RAT in my wardrobe made a hole,
Gnawing a waistcoat and two pairs of breeches
    Besides six handkerchiefs, upon my soul !
Ye tender fair, who to the rescue rushed,
Right well you mended them although you blushed !

19

What more have I to add ?—Strong baffling winds
    Delay our progress but prolong our joys ;
Meantime my heart sweet consolation finds,
    While sage philosophy my mind employs.
Who could be dull in such divine society ?
I could live thus for years without satiety.

Down the Nile.

(*Continued.*)

—o—

20

With Egypt's oldest relics of times past,
    Famed Memphis and Sakkara, we wound up
For a *bonne-bouche*, reserved until the last,
    As folk oft keep *tit-bits* whereon to sup ;
Though we saw naught at Memphis, I must say,
Save some old sculptures scattered on the way.

21

But, lying in a low and shady spot,
    Like a big Brobdignagian in his sleep,
We saw great Rameses,* his royal face
    Calm and composed, as though in slumber deep ;

---

* This refers to the magnificent fragment of Rameses the Great at Memphis, which was presented many years ago to the British Government, but has been suffered to lie neglected in a pit, owing to the great cost its transport to England would involve. Wilkinson describing it, says : "The expression of the face, which is perfectly preserved, is very beautiful."

His lips submissively the cold clay press,
Teaching from age to age man's littleness.

22

Had stiff-necked PHARAOH, in his generation,
    Wisely succumbed to the Divine command,
Egypt might still retain a foremost station,
    And MEMPHIS in its ancient grandeur stand ;
Such was the sermon preached by those old stones
To bring proud man down on his marrow-bones.

23

Passing SAKKARA'S terraced pyramid,
    We saw the "GROTTO OF THE SACRED BULL,"
Where, in sarcophagus, each corpse was hid,
    In days when beasts were gods, and earth was
        full
Of superstition, such as makes us glad
That we were born in times not quite so bad.

.   .   .

24

FINIS !   Here terminates our Nile career !
    The "Pleiades" no more at mess shall muster ;
Naught will remain to us save memories dear,
    Which in each breast henceforth will fondly
        cluster ;

While our Nile voyage, with its interests rife,
Will seem like a bright OASIS in life.

25

The " Star of India," proved a happy home,
   Wherein no note of discord ever entered ;
And now, the hour of separation come,
   We find our heart's best feelings in it centered.
Thus smoothly down life's current may we glide,
Then meet to part no more, *" Heaven's light our*
      *guide."**

26

Nor be forgotten our good DRAGOMAN,
   Who liberally all our wants supplied ;
Let us indulgently his foibles scan ;
   To make things pleasant to us all he tried :
We wish him future luck in his profession,
Till he has wealth enough in his possession.

27

NICOLAI also was a worthy wight,
   " All things to all," especially the fair,
Who viewed his handsome person with delight,
   Deeming him an Adonis in his air :

---

* *" Heaven's light our guide"* is the motto of the Order of the
"Star of India."

At meals he dutifully served each dear,
Oft whispering Arab lessons in her ear.

28

What shall I say of little Benjamin,
    Our ugly, impish, wide-mouthed Nubian boy ?
Whom, fascinated by his coal-black skin,
    The ladies made their special pet and toy ;
Clothed him in purple to his own surprise,
Then called him in to brush away the flies.

29

It fared not thus with our poor household fag,
    Elias, best abused of all on board ;
From morn till eve he ne'er was seen to flag ;
    By each in turn his name was loudly roared ;
He ironed clothes, made beds, at meals attended,
Yet seldom was with female smiles befriended.

30

Lastly, our faithful *Rais** and trusty crew,
    The skilful navigators of our boat,
Must have the grateful tribute justly due ;
    Right well they laboured, and kept us afloat,

---

* Arabic term for a " ship's captain.'

Free from all rocks and sandbanks wisely steer-
  ing,
And with melodious strains our spirits cheering.

. . . .

31

And now, farewell ! a word that must be spoken
  Sooner or later by each living soul.
Receive these parting stanzas as a token
  From one who would his humble name enrol
In your choice list of absent friends most cherished,
Even when his worthless body shall have perished.

The Great Petrified Forest.

(*A Vision of the Desert.*)

—o—

[Having, during our stay at Cairo, read a somewhat sensational
account in the *London Illustrated News* of a newly discovered
"petrified forest" about ten miles west of the great pyramids,
we were induced to visit the locality.   Another so-called
"petrified forest" has long been known to travellers on the
eastern bank of the Nile, within a morning's ride from Cairo ;
but the large specimens have long ago nearly all disappeared
under the exhaustive chisels of curiosity hunters ; whereas we
were now led to believe in the existence of a real park of entire
trees, standing *in situ*, where they had originally grown.]

I

ALL ye who annually flock to Cairo,
  Of whatsoe'er profession, sex, or age,
To see the wonders of the land of Pharaoh,
  And with antiquity your mind engage ;
Yield an attentive ear unto my lay,
Whilst I rehearse the marvels of a day.

2

One morn, the thirst for knowledge to appease,
  Three sage philosophers from Cairo started,
[For wise folk somehow always pack in *threes,*]
  And to the Pyramids in hurry darted ;
One was an Artist of no meagre fame ;
The other two, a General and his dame.

3

'Twas whispered that far off, in desert wild,
  Stood a primeval forest turned to stone ;
So thus, by curiosity beguiled,
  This sapient trio zealously had gone
To sketch and scrutinise the new-found mystery,
And to the ignorant unfold its history.

4

Behold us, then (for I was of the party),
  Pausing 'neath CHEOPS' pyramidal shade,
Each on his donkey, resolute and hearty,
  Ready to rush wherever fancy bade ;
To the far west we strained our eager gaze,
And saw a vision floating through the haze.

5

Lo ! at a mountain's base, in gaunt array,
  Like giant sentinels around a throne,

A thousand stately trees their trunks display,
 Each motionless and rigid as a stone !
Such was the " Fossil forest " fancy drew ;
Who could say whether it were false or true ?

6

Forward we plunged into the desert drear ;
 A trackless sandy waste before us spread ;
Old CHEOPS melted dimly in our rear,
 As o'er some sea's vast void we seemed to tread ;
And still imagination played its prank,
Like a *mirage*, and filled the distant blank,—

7

Picturing fossil nests on every bough,
 Each filled with fossil eggs and fossil birds,
For even the wisest men at times, somehow,
 Love to delude themselves with flattering words ;
And liken geese to swans, pebbles to pearls,
Whilst the wild brain in pleased confusion whirls.

8

Thus, then, it was, we hugged the dear delusion,
 Until our guide announced our journey ended,
And pointed grimly out, to our confusion,
 Two prostrate trunks along the sand extended ;

These were the " Fossil forest," he avowed,
And seemed of the great fact immensely proud.

9

Not quite so *we !*   Staring, we stood aghast,
　　Reluctant each his pent-up thoughts to utter ;
But famished nature urging a repast,
　　We turned for comfort to our bread and butter.
" What went ye in the desert waste to see ? "
" Don't you feel rather *up a fossil tree ?* "

Anathema to the Flies of Egypt.

—o—

[This enduring bequest of Moses may be considered the only real
  drawback to enjoyment on the Nile, and certainly renders
  the great Jewish lawyer somewhat unpopular with modern
  travellers. The following lines may be considered a final out-
  burst of pent-up wrath at the end of a two months' trip, which
  was otherwise a period of perfect delight to us all.]

CONFOUND those odious flies !
How they do tantalise,
Hovering round my eyes,
    Tickling my nose,
Causing me oft to sneeze,
Giving no rest or ease,
Ever in wait to teaze,
    Meanest of foes !
What do you want, you beast !
Pest of all in the East ;
Go somewhere else to feast,
    Get away, do !

Leave in peace my poor head ;
On yonder slice of bread
You 'll find some honey spread,
     Nicer for you !
Ah ! big botheration
And loud execration
To Egypt's old nation
     For angering Moses !
Bringing such plagues on man ;
Rest well he never can,
Pestered by insect clan
     While he reposes.
But, worst of all, ye flies !
Your race my temper tries ;
     Oh, how I hate you !
How could Nature, I wonder,
Commit such a blunder
     As to create you !

PART II.

—◆—

LAYS OF WONDER-LAND.

Up a Tree !

(A Real Adventure.)

—o—

1

IT happened sixteen years ago—
　It seems but yesterday to me ;
And still, as back my thoughts I throw,
It sets my heart all in a glow,
　That vision in a cherry-tree !

2

For on a lofty branch I saw,
　Enthroned amid the sheltering shade,
Crowned with a mushroom hat of straw,
Looking like one whose will was law,
　A most bewildering young maid.

3

Like veritable " Fairy Queen,"
　Surrounded by her little court
Of elfin forms, she sate serene ;
So sweet a group I ne'er had seen,
　Nor one so ripe for merry sport.

4

As though to check my bold advance,
  She flashed on me her lustrous eyes ;
Forthwith I felt their lightning glance
With magnet's force my soul entrance ;
  Rooted I stood in glad surprise.

5

Anon, o'er her sweet lips there stole
  A playful and bewitching smile ;
Then, in the rapture of my soul,
I seemed to see Love's very goal,
  Such power hath Beauty to beguile !

6

Up to this fairy's tempting bower
  A friendly ladder seemed to lead ;
I placed my foot with manful power
On the first step, when, lo ! a shower
  Of cherries fell upon my head.

7

Like startled bees their queen who guard,
  I saw each young elf's arm upraised ;
Cherries, like hail, fell fast and hard
Full on the face of this poor Bard,
  As still he upward strode amazed.

8

The goal was gained !   On a spare bough
  I innocently took my seat ;
But short my triumph proved,—for now
My hat she knocked from off my brow,
  While laughing elves approved the feat.

9

Thus challenged by my fairy foe,
  I made a dash at her broad brim,
And tossed it to the earth below ;
Her face flushed up with crimson glow,
  Her long loose hair all out of trim !

10

Then came a friendly mutual truce,
  And fruits of victory were mine ;
My lips were stained with cherry juice ;
But oft I wondered who the deuce
  Could be this unknown nymph divine.

11

She too would know from whence I came,
  Like one of the sky's wandering stars ;
What my profession, age, and name ?
Each word she uttered fanned a flame
  Like that which Venus lit in Mars.

12

Methought till then I ne'er had met
    Such a delicious little creature,
So wild and frolicsome, and yet
So clever, nice, and sweet a pet;
    So perfect too in every feature!

13

At last 'twas time to end our chat,
    And down the ladder we descended;
Forthwith she pounced on my poor hat,
Then bounded off like a wild cat,
    Whilst I behind her close attended.

14

The pace was perilous and fast,
    And oft she doubled like a hare.
But to a halt she came at last,
Then round her both my arms I cast,
    And would have kissed her if I dare.

15

But, at this crisis, up there rushed
    A horrid nursery-governess!
My fair one's hat was sadly crushed,
She gave me one last look and blushed,
    Then left me standing in distress.

16

'Twas thus my vision came and fled !
  The little coquette ! what cared *she ?*
We met when sixteen years had sped,
And both had long been *mar-ri-ed ;*
  But she had not forgotten me ;
  And still she was most fair to see,
  My charmer of the cherry-tree !

La Grande Chartreuse.

(*A True Story.*)

—o—

[This celebrated convent is romantically situated on the summit of a
mountain in Dauphiné, nearly 5000 feet above the sea. It was
first erected by St Bruno, A. D. 1080, in obedience to whose strin-
gent rules no female was allowed during seven centuries to tread
within five miles of the sanctuary. It has long been famous
for the excellent liqueur manufactured by the monks.]

I

I HAVE a truthful tale to tell
(No unsubstantial dream),
Of what myself and spouse befell
By midnight in a mountain dell—
An awe-inspiring theme !

2

Prompted by Eve's primeval greed .
Forbidden fruit to gobble,
One morn we started off full speed
In a chaise drawn by one lank steed,
Which just contrived to hobble.

3

Full fifteen miles this quadruped
    Managed his load to drag ;
Then coming to a stand-still dead,
He would not budge an inch till fed,
    So was allowed to lag.

4

Fifteen more miles we onward went
    To a big mountain's base,
And as our horse's power was spent,
We stopped, by no means malcontent,
    Some *déjeûner* to face.

5

Veal cutlets, beans, potatoes, trout,
    We soon contrived to swallow,
Which made us feel quite strong and stout,
So boldly we again set out
    The steep ascent to follow.

6

For lo ! on this same mountain top
    Our pilgrimage must end ;
'Twas there we meant all night to stop,
Unless sent flying, neck and crop,
    By some unfriendly friend.

7

'Tis time that I should now explain
  That to yon lone retreat
St Bruno fled, but fled in vain,
That never in this world again
  He female form might meet.

8

And there he formed a brotherhood,
  Fierce *Woman-haters* all,
Who, in their efforts to be good,
Stinted the flesh with scanty food,
  Mindful of Adam's fall.

9

For centuries no petticoat
  Could pierce that sacred fold ;
Frail curiosity to gloat
'Mid matrimony's antidote
  None then was found so bold.

10

But now, alas ! excursion trains
  And other aids of travel
Have quite outwitted Bruno's brains ;
Women in crowds forsake the plains
  The mystery to unravel.

11

'Tis an incentive to their zeal
  To think it fruit forbidden ;
To " woman's rights " they now appeal,
And to the blushing monks reveal
  Their varied charms unchidden.

12

The mount's wild gorge they penetrate,
  Careless of toil they clamber ;
They throng outside the convent gate,
Making each monk deplore his fate,
  And linger in his chamber.

13

My spouse, as curious as the rest,
  Had long urged this excursion ;
And as we neared the saintly nest
Loudly her inward joy expressed,
  Deeming it huge diversion.

14

A meek monk on the road we passed,
  Who turned away his head,
Telling his beads furious and fast,
As though each moment were his last,
  So full was he of dread.

15

Of female form the very rustle
 To him was diabolic,
With Satan's self he seemed to tussle,
And out of harm's way tried to bustle,
 Like one who feared the cholic.

16

Our upward path seemed formed to be
 Nature's own royal portal,
Leading, through scenes of majesty,
To some vast height where men might see
 The throne of the Immortal!

17

" Excelsior!" we reached at last
 The convent's awful gate;
We rang the bell; a monk aghast
Poked out his head, and one glance cast
 Of horror at my mate.

18

" No women here allowed 1 " he cried,
 "But yonder you may find
A house wherein some nuns abide;
There, for one night, your wife may hide,
 And meet with treatment kind."

19

Thus having spoke, he closed the door;
  We sought and found a nun ;
The place seemed desolate and poor,
But of a bed the dame made sure,
  Though I still wanted one.

20

So back to the good monk I sped,
  To make my meek demand ;
To a small cell was straightway led,
Was told the hour when guests were fed,
  Then took my key in hand.

21

Within the hall were grouped a score
  Of worldlings like to me;
With them I was conducted o'er
Through many a mazy corridor,
  To see what we might see.

22

This was not much ;—some books quite old ;
  Queer pictures ; chapels ; cells ;
Gravestones of monks long turned to mould ;
Such things their own quaint story told
  As plain as the church-bells.

23

Then, sauntering forth, I sought the dame,
  And through the woods we wended
Until the hour for parting came ;
Nor need you deem me much to blame
  If here my story *ended*.

24

But here, in truth, it doth *begin !*
  For off I went to dinner,
Which seemed a penance for past sin,
A speedy mode of getting thin,
  And, after each meal, thinner !

25

At least I thought so, till at last
  They gave me some "*liqueur*,"
So good, I soon forgot the past,
And thought it quite worth while to fast,
  Such finish to ensure.

26

I licked my lips, and longed for more !
  Come to my aid, O muse !
Inspire me while the praise I roar
Of that sweet stuff I now outpour,
  My own beloved "CHARTREUSE !"

27

I sought my humble cell at nine,
   And tumbled into bed ;
I felt within a glow benign ;
A halo round me seemed to shine,
   Like that round some saint's head.

28

I sank into a sleep profound ;
   Perhaps I may have *snored ;*
What matter ?—No wife heard the sound,
Nor tossed me out on the hard ground,
   Or the floor's harder board.

29

I slept ;—till, hark !—I hear the toll
   Of a most dismal bell ;
It seems to harrow up my soul ;
So underneath the sheets I roll
   To smother the dread knell.

30

But all in vain !—Sweet rest has fled ;
   The clock proclaims midnight ;

The thought occurs that MASS is said *
At that strange hour,—so out of bed
  I start, and strike a light.

31

In haste I dress ; then sally out
  To seek my way to church ;
Dark corridors I grope about
Until I feel inclined to shout,
  So hopeless seems my search.

32

I hear the distant voice of monk
  In melancholy chaunt,
Then all seems in deep silence sunk,
And I begin to feel a funk,
  And ghosts my fancy haunt.

33

I long to get back to my room,
  But feel lost in a maze
Of galleries involved in gloom,
Until methinks it is my doom
  Therein to end my days.

---

* The English Guide-books designate as a midnight "Mass"
what is, correctly speaking, only "Matins."

34

At length I spy a light afar,
  An old monk's flickering taper ;
I hail it as my guiding-star,
And knock my head against a bar
  While towards it swift I caper.

35

Bound by his strict vow *not to talk*,
  The monk makes sundry signs
In which direction I should walk,
So off accordingly I stalk
  To where a dim light shines.

36

Once more I hear the solemn strain
  Of voices chaunting prayer ;
I stumble on a door, and strain
My back in striving to obtain
  An entrance then and there.

37

At last, to end my story queer,
  A man came to my aid,
And took me where I well might *hear*,
But could *see* nothing very clear,
  Nor tell a monk from maid.

38

For a whole hour the dismal tones
 Monotonously solemn,
Like the wind's solitary moans,
Or river rolling over stones,
 I heard behind a column.

39

Then, growing desperate, once more
 I sought my own small cell ;
And tried the darkness to explore,
Losing my bearings o'er and o'er ;—
 But "all 's well that ends well."

40

My bed I gained. The monks' dull drawl
 Acted like soporific ;
Soundly I slept till the bell's call
To chapel once more summoned all,
 With clanging quite terrific.

41

I dressed, and bought a good supply
 Of " Chartreuse " famous tipple ;
The dame soon at it cocked her eye,
As though she longed at once to try
 Its pleasant inward ripple.

42

In the nuns' house 'twas the hard law
  No husband there might rest,
Nor touch provisions with his paw,
Still less upon them use his jaw
  To cause them to digest !

43

Nevertheless, this rule to break,
  My dame used coaxing wile ;
So I got leave some food to take
Quite on the sly, for pure love's sake,
  By means of harmless guile.

44

'Twas managed thus : while none could spy
  I quietly was smuggled
Into a sweet nun's cell close by,
[*She* was not there, unluckily !]
  And so the monks were juggled.

45

Thither the nuns some coffee bore
  My inward man to nourish,
While one kept watch outside the door ;
The generous creatures I adore !
  Long may they live and flourish !

46

And now at last my tale is told,
  For homeward we then turned,
Leaving behind a little gold
For BRUNO'S sake and convent old,
  Which had our good-will earned.

47

For though sweet woman they abuse,
  This world is much their debtor,
Were it but for their good "Chartreuse,"
And the warm glow it doth diffuse,
  Whereby men are made better.

48

Then let us drink to Bruno's health
  In a mellifluous bumper
Of his own brew ! his convent's wealth,
Whose godly monks do good by stealth ;
  So give the board a thumper !

The Magic Mushroom.

(A Fairy Tale founded on fact.)

—o—

1

I WILL a wondrous story tell
  To all who wish to know,
Of something that myself befell
  While wintering at Pau.

2

Now Pau 's a town in Southern France,
  Close to the Pyrenees,
Where English people go to dance
  And do what else they please.

3

But let me caution each male friend,
  Young, middle-aged, and old,
Who thither may propose to wend,
  'Gainst perils manifold.

4

For, let him go where'er he may,
  To foxhunt, band, or church,
Fair damsels will fall in his way,
  Without the need to search.

5

And such bewitching creatures, too,
  That, without any flattery,
Each pair of eyes the work will do
  Of an entire field-battery !

6

For me, although a married man,
  And all unused to flirt,
Quite comprehend I never can
  How I escaped unhurt.

7

But to resume my truthful tale :
  One day I went to sketch
A scene where, far beyond the vale,
  The snow-clad mountains stretch ;

8

And spying a snug shady spot
  Beneath some spreading trees,

The sun's rays waxing somewhat hot,
  I there reclined at ease.

9

And might have, doubtless, in due time,
  Done something worth a prize,
But for a spectacle sublime
  That met my wondering eyes.

10

For underneath a neighbouring tree,
  Like huge umbrella spread,
I could discern what seemed to be
  A giant mushroom's head.

11

Now fungi, as we all well know,
  By fairies oft are haunted,
And hoping still to find it so,
  I towards it strode undaunted.

12

Thinks I, of mushrooms this must be
  The king, and hence, I guess,
Of fairies all I soon shall see
  The queen, and nothing less.

13

Approaching near, and nearer still,
  To this botanic wonder,
Conceive the gratifying thrill
  I felt, when, peeping under,

14

I saw disclosed, in beauty clad,
  The loveliest of faces ;
Oh ! 'twas enough to drive me mad,
  That paragon of graces !

15

I stood awhile like one amazed
  Or in mesmeric trance,
And still in rapture's spell I gazed,
  Nor farther could advance.

16

Till suddenly there stole a smile
  O'er her mellifluous mouth ;
Oh ! 'twas worth travelling many a mile
  To see, from North to South !

17

And, turning up her lustrous eyes,
  She gave me such a look

As even poet's brain defies
　To tell of in a book.

18

Encouraged thus to feel at ease,
　I gently took her hand,
And soon I felt its kindly squeeze
　Restore my self-command.

19

I spied a volume in her lap,
　And timidly inquired
The name of the thrice-lucky chap
　Whose verse her feelings fired.

20

It proved to be a German bard,
　Whose name I could not utter;
At least to do so would be hard
　Without a deal of splutter.

21

I asked her favourite work in prose;
　And (could I be mistaken?)
Cocking aloft her pretty nose,
　She promptly answered, " BACON."

22

At that great name I felt my head
　Grow numb as pickled salmon ;
And scarcely knowing what I said,
　Exclaimed abruptly, "GAMMON !"

23

She shrieked ! I fainted on the spot,
　And lay like one quite dead ;
Coming to life, I found her not—
　My Fairy Queen had fled !

24

But on the sacred spot of ground
　Where she so lately sat,
The Mushroom there transformed I found
　Into a monster HAT !

25

Months glided on, I scarce knew how ;
　One object filled my brain—
That Heaven would kindly me allow
　To see her once again.

26

Last week, a little before dark,
　When daylight downward dips,

I caught a brief glimpse in the Park
   Of those loved eyes and lips.

27

I rushed on madly through the crowd,
   Who tried my coat to grab,
I shouted out in accents loud ;
   She—vanished in a cab !

28

Still it was joy to feel her nigh,
   To breathe the same sweet air ;
And I acknowledged with a sigh
   That Heaven had heard my prayer.

29

Once more we met : in virgin white
   She seemed arrayed for cloister ;
But oh ! the horror of the sight !
   She clutched a huge fat oyster !

30

Her eyes, dilating, beamed with bliss,
   Her jaws she opened wide,
And down the fathomless abyss
   I saw the monster glide.

31

What happened next I cannot tell ;
A film came o'er each eye ;
Vision of Fairy-land, farewell !
Alas ! it's all a lie !

Up in the Clouds.

(*A Valentine.*)

—o—

1

I DREAMT—alas ! 'twas but a dream—
I was in a balloon,
Which in its upward course did seem
To travel towards the moon.

2

And in the car along with me
Were three angelic creatures,
Whom I discovered soon to be
Perfect in form and features.

3

I thought what sport we would enjoy
Together in the clouds,
Free from the noise and base alloy
Of vulgar earthly crowds.

4

And as we up and up advanced,
We now and then peeped down,

And through our opera glasses glanced
　　Upon Boulogne's fair town.

5

Outside a house in " Rue l'Ecu "
　　We spied a female mob
Gazing at a good man and true,
　　Who seemed to sit and sob.

6

I marvelled why so good a man
　　Should thus sit down to cry ;
And my companions began
　　To look ashamed and sigh.

7

Then suddenly I recognised
　　Their once familiar faces
As those of friends most highly prized—
　　My own " three Boulogne graces ! "

8

Forthwith I scribbled a brief note :
　　" Dear friend ! don't be alarmed ;
The relatives on whom you doat
　　Are safe—and won't be harmed.

9

"They 're only going to the moon
  To get a change of air ;
I 'll bring back to you very soon
  Each pretty truant fair ! "

10

I dropped the note, and saw it fall
  Close to his very toes ;
Which made him start, and loudly bawl,
  And cock aloft his nose.

11

He raised his hands in great amaze,
  His wife waved hers to him ;
Then we got shrouded in a haze,
  And all around grew dim !

12

So, having nothing else to do,
  Pray deem it not amiss
If I confess ('twixt me and you)
  I gave each one—a kiss !

13

The dear things thought it no more crime
  Than though I were their brother ;

And then, to while away the time,
  Each gave to me—another!

14

So thus, lost in the clouds, we passed
  A very happy hour;
But such joys were too sweet to last,
  Without soon turning sour.

15

For lo! as we drew near the moon,
  A wandering star rushed out,
And tore the silk of our balloon,
  And put us all to rout!

16

What next befell I cannot say,
  But I awoke in bed,
And then found out, to my dismay,
  A bandage round my head.

17

I long to learn how matters fare
  With my companions three,
But to my wife I would not dare
  Reveal my little spree!

A "*Farewell*" at Pau.

I

Maiden! yon soaring eagle mark!
I would that I were he,
And you a lively little lark;
How happy we might be!

2

I 'd pounce upon you in the sky
While practising your hymn,
And to some lofty peak I 'd fly,
To some nook snug and trim.

3

I would not eat you, lovely maid!
For that I 'm much too wary;
But I 'd invoke the timely aid
Of some kind-hearted fairy;

4

And you should be once more a girl,
    In dainty gauze decked out,
And I a youth ; oh! then we'd whirl
    And waltz all round about.

5

We'd have no need of fife or fiddle
    To tantalise our ears ;
Enough for us to solve the riddle,
    The "music of the spheres !"

6

When tired of dancing, we'd seek out
    Some cascade's glittering spray,
And there we'd promenade about
    Upon the rainbow's ray.

7

Our fare should be roast butterfly,
    Served up with "Sauce of kisses ;"
And, as we sat at meals we'd cry,
    "Oh ! this most perfect bliss is !"

8

Alas ! can this be all a dream ?
    And are we still at Pau ?

And do I hear the engine's scream ?
  And are you going to go ?

9

Stern is the fact, I fear, and true ;
  My vision 's at an end !
Then take, dear maid ! this fond adieu
  From your lamenting friend.

10

Henceforth the lark's note in the sky
  Will seem to sing of *thee ;*
Say, when Jove's soaring bird you spy,
  Will you too think of *me ?*

An Early Visitor.

(Written in reply to a Valentine.)

— ο —

1

THIS morn, on waking from my nap,
I heard a little gentle tap
        At my room door ;
A pretty boy with curly head
Peeped in and tossed upon my bed
        A note he bore.

2

He had a bow with silver strings,
And wore a pair of tiny wings,
        Also a quiver ;
But deuce a garment did he wear,
And the sight of his body bare
        Quite made one shiver.

3

But while the note perusing, lo !
I suddenly felt in a glow,
  And through my heart
There darted an electric thrill ;
And I experience a pain still
  Just in that part !

4

I looked, and lo ! that naughty boy
Stood there, no longer meek and coy,
  But in his hand
He poised his bow, and aimed an arrow
Right at my heart's most vital marrow,
  Smiling quite bland.

5

I bounced from bed ; he turned his back ;
I gave it a resounding smack,
  Whereat he started ;
His nether limbs, too, seemed to wriggle,
Then, uttering a joyous giggle,
  Away he darted !

6

Alas! the urchin was too quick!
His shaft he had contrived to stick
    In my heart's core.
Oh dear! oh dear! what shall I do?
Perhaps some kind nymph such as you
    Will heal my sore!

A Voice from "Les Eaux Bonnes" in the Pyrenees.

—o—

1

UNTIRINGLY upon yon peaks I gaze,
  Whose snow-clad summits pierce the calm blue
    sky,
Sheltered the while from glowing noonday blaze
  'Neath some grand rock, with cool stream dash-
    ing by.

2

Yon virgin snow, on azure bed reposing,
  Tells us of heaven's own purity and truth,
Each passing moment some new phase disclosing
  Of glorified and everlasting youth.

3

In what stern contrast frowns the bold bare mass
  Of dizzy steep! making us pigmies wonder
How such catastrophe could come to pass
  When this old Earth was rudely rent asunder ;

4

While at its base swells many a verdant slope,
    Arrayed in varied garb of smiling green,
Encouraging each drooping heart to hope,
    And 'mid life's shocks maintain a front serene.

5

Here, hemmed in by huge rocky mountain piles,
    Like Venus in old Vulcan's rough embraces,
"Eaux Bonnes" each welcome traveller beguiles—
    Justly esteemed a paradise of places.

6

Methinks no Paris milliner can vie
    With old Dame NATURE—in form, colour, taste,
She beats them all! Let then Eve's daughters try
    Her skill, nor so much wealth on rubbish waste!

A SOUVENIR OF VENICE.—*Page 67*

A Souvenir of Venice.

—o—

1

"I stood at Venice"—[here I quote Lord Byron]—
Upon an ancient bridge of goodly size,
And viewed therefrom the structures that environ
The Grand Canal, and fascinate the eyes
Of strangers, taking lazy exercise
In gondolas, reclining quite at ease ;
Their minds, meanwhile, striving to realise
The amphibious lives of those lords of the seas,
Whose relics still possess such wondrous power to
    please.

2

They must have been grand fellows in their way,
Those grim old Doges—sworn foes of all Turks
And heretics ; oft exercising ruthless sway,
And somewhat overprompt to use their dirks ;

But lavish patrons of Art's glorious works,
Which still survive for us—their sole bequest—
Amid the scenes where Titian's spirit lurks:
In their huge marble tombs long may they rest
In undisturbed repose—their memory not unblest!

3

For poets, like myself, painters, and all
Who wander here and there in search of beauty,
Venice is still a Venus, to enthral
The senses, and entice from sterner duty
Awaiting us in London's region sooty.
Oh! I could sit enthralled for hours, and gaze
On yon superb pile styled "Della Salute,"
Or watching Dame Fortuna's* fickle ways,
As she with outstretched skirt each varying breeze
      betrays.

4

But would you view the scene in all its glory,
Forget not, on some clear and sunny day,
To mount the tower of " Giorgio Maggiore,"
And see below you spread, in bright array,

---

* The weather-vane on the Dogana tower is a figure of " Fortuna "
spreading out a very flimsy garment to catch the breeze.

Each isle and inlet of the beauteous bay ;
And, in the midst, Old Ocean's quondam Bride,
With her attendant nymphs, almost as gay,
To outward seeming, as when, in her pride
She reigned a mighty queen, and every foe defied !

5

I might perhaps have said more in her praise
But for this morning's unexpected blow ;
When, gazing forth for the sun's genial rays,
I saw instead—a storm of pelting snow !*
In Venice a most rare event, I trow ;
But it has struck a chill into my heart,
And frozen up my poem's fervid flow.
Venice ! farewell !—All lovely as thou art,
Oh ! that in such cold guise our lot should be to
    part !

* This refers to a snowstorm of extraordinary severity which
occurred in October 1869.

Monte Rosa, from Macugnaga.

[Macugnaga is one of the loveliest spots in the Alps, at the foot of
Monte Rosa, on the Italian side.]

QUEEN of the Alps! thy battlemented crest *
Like a huge hydra rears its many heads,
Defiant as a fortress;—thy long rest
Through countless ages, 'mid pure snowy beds,
Was undisturbed by prying gaze of man;
Or if defiled by his presumptuous tread,
Thy vengeance swift destroyed his daring plan,
Pouring dread avalanches o'er his head,
Sweeping him from thee like a noxious thing !
But now, man's turn of triumph has begun ;
No longer need he yield to queen or king,
And royalty, e'en here, its race has run.
But beauty such as thine shall ever reign
Within our hearts, nor be unveiled in vain !

---

  * The Rev. S. W. King, in his " Italian Valleys of the Pennine
Alps," says regarding Monte Rosa, "The many summits may be
compared to the battlements of an immense bastion of snow alps."

MONTE ROSA.—*Page* 100.

Vaucluse.

(An Acrostic Sonnet, composed in Petrarch's Garden.)

———o———

[Vaucluse is about sixteen miles from Avignon, and was the favourite
abode of Petrarch.]

P II.GRIMS of love, we sought this famed retreat,
E ager to taste its consecrated flood,
T hat saw so oft Petrarch his Laura greet ;
R eflecting both, as on its brink they stood
A dmiring nature much, each other *most ;*
R ecounting o'er and o'er affection's tale ;
C reating their own world in this sweet vale, [boast!
A t once the poet's theme and true love's endless

E mpires and centuries have passed away,

L eaving behind them wrecks of human madness ;
A nd still, with feelings fresh as flowers of May,
U nto this Poet's haunt we hie with gladness,
R eciting his fond verse, his faults forgiving,
A s best incentive to all faithful lovers living !

Ascent of the Rigi.

—o—

[Having read in "Murray" that a book was kept in the Rigi,
wherein travellers were invited to record their feelings in verse,
these lines were composed with that object ; but I found the
book had disappeared soon after the establishment of railways
in Switzerland.]

1

FRIENDS, Britons, countrymen! I don't pretend
    To be a poet born ; but 'tis the duty
Of all men who this mountain top ascend
    To celebrate in verse its varied beauty ;
So, not to be behindhand in my zeal,
I seize my pen to utter all I feel.

2

And to begin ; let me at once declare
    My satisfaction to have reached the top,
Along those nine miles of continuous stair,
    That seemed as though it never meant to stop ;
But since to climb the Rigi is the fashion,
It 's no use putting one's self in a passion.

3

Thank heaven! the deed is done ; and here I stand,
   Surveying, like a map, the world below ;
Yon giant Alps uplift their summits grand,
   Poking sharp snouts from beds of dazzling snow ;
Below, a perfect maze of lakes and valleys—
All which with " Murray's Handbook " truly tallies.

4

In fact, therein you 'll find, completely booked,
   The fullest details of the Rigi tale ;
All that e'en poet's brain has ever cooked ;
   To rival which my own poor powers might fail ;
Therefore, to save my readers from the worry,
I 'll wind up by referring them to " Murray."

A Perilous Ascent of the Ortler-Spitz.

(Dedicated to the Alpine Club.)

—o—

[Having perused in the Hotel book at Trafoi, on Mount Stelvio,
sundry magniloquent descriptions, by members of the Alpine
Club, of their wonderful ascents of the "Ortler-Spitz," I felt
an irresistible ambition to surpass them all, and the following
remarkable results rewarded my efforts.]

HAVING read all the records in the book,
And swallowed all the choice viands of the cook,
I smoked a pipe, and felt forthwith inspired
To climb the "Ortler." Meanwhile, being tired,
I went to bed, resolved to rise at three
And start, without a guide, upon this spree.

.   .   .   .   .

Somehow, my sleep was troubled; visions drear
Of grim old DOLOMITES, with shapes most queer,
Like ghostly giants hovered round the room,
And seemed to beckon me to share their doom :

My wife declared I snored !   I don't believe her ;
For, was not woman ever man's deceiver?

   .   .   .   .   .

At three precisely from repose I started,
And on my glorious heavenward course departed ;
Stowing some bread and brandy in my pocket,
Off I rushed upward like a signal rocket ;
Nor once looked back, nor pretext found to stop,
Until I reached the very tipmost top !
 Glaciers and precipices all in vain
Opposed my path ; nought could my feet detain ;
Not Beelzebub himself could my mad march
     restrain !

   .   .   .   .   .

Hurrah ! at last on Ortler's snow-capped pate
I stood alone !   My happiness was great !
Balanced on tiptoe to enjoy the view,
I crowed in triumph—" *Cock-a-doodle-doo !* "
Alas ! just then my foot slipped in the snow ;
Headlong I fell down the abyss below !
My senses fled !   .   .   .   .
     .   .   Crash ! .   .   .
     .   .   .   Waking, lo ! I found
My poor old carcass sprawling on the ground ;

And peering round through the dim morning gloom,
Methought I recognised the inn's small room;
While, judging from the bruises on my head,
'Twould seem that I had—*tumbled out of bed !*

.   .   .   .   .

Still, to all honest minds endowed with reason,
Mine must be deemed *the* ascent of the season !

Ober-Ammergau.

(*September* 1871.)

—*o*—

BOUND by ancestral solemn vows
   Peculiar to the place,
Kind Heav'n this rustic folk endows
   With every needful grace.

'Mid Alpine wilds remote they dwell,
   Far from the world's highways,
Summoned each morning by church bell
   To sing their Maker's praise.

'Tis their high privilege and glory
   Christ's sufferings to relate,
And re-enact that wondrous story
   Whereon depends our fate.

'Tis theirs, in this degenerate age,
   Of scoffing unbelief,
To illustrate each holy page
   That tells our Saviour's grief;

By living pictures to recall
  His love and lingering death,
When, to redeem us from our fall,
  He yielded up his breath.

This wayward world has heard once more
  God's word from peasant's mouth ;
Crowds gathered round the cottage door
  From north, east, west, and south.

Tourists by thousands rushed to gaze
  And coldly criticise,
But few, alas ! will mend their ways
  Or the great lesson prize.

Yet may these simple preachers long
  Persist, on this world's stage,
To teach mankind by play and song
  Christ's love from age to age !

Farewell Acrostic to Ober-Ammergau.

(September 1871.)

—o—

O BLEST retreat for faith, heartfelt and sound !
B anished from courts and cities, in this vale
E mbosomed, Christian piety hath found
R efuge in souls where no dark doubts assail.

A mid these mountains shines a Beacon* bright,
M aking the sceptic's flickering torch obscure !
M ultitudes throng to hail its heavenly light ;
E arth hears once more God's wisdom from the poor.
R eceive the thanks of one who hath been taught
G reat truths that oft lie hidden from the wise ;
A dieu ! all ye who have such marvel wrought,
U ntil the last loud trump shall bid us rise !

* The point of this lay partly in the fact that a beacon-light was kindled every night, during the performance of the Passion Play, on the lofty mountain crag which overhangs the village.

The Old Stones of Rome.

(A Lent Lecture, written at Rome.)

—o—

WHAT apter text for lecture can be found
Than that which meets us here while gazing round!
What hidden stores of eloquence and learning
Do Rome's old stones divulge to minds discerning !
What wondrous echoes from far distant ages
Haunt her abodes of senators and sages ;
Telling how great states rose, declined, and crum-
    bled ;
How heroes were made gods, and tyrants humbled !
Kingdoms, republics, empires,—each in turn
Fulfilling their own times ; till all should learn
Man's insignificance,—Jehovah's might,—
And lean on HIS strong arm who guards the right.

Here, amid desolation more profound
By contrast with the living world around,
Majestic still, in ruined glory, lies
That once proud mistress of earth's destinies,
The city of the Cæsars !—Here we trace
The classic haunts of those whose memories grace

Immortal history ;—men whose magic names
Shine through all time; giants whose grandeur
    shames
Us modern pigmies; so that we still mount
For inspiration to the parent fount
Whence Wisdom first, with Freedom in its wake,
Gushed forth, the bounds of ignorance to break ;
And in the dark depths of whose classic stream
We still may dive for many a wholesome theme
Wherewith to dose our colleges and schools,
Spiced·well with rods to lash the backs of fools.

Here, too, great Cæsar triumphed !—Noblest he
Of Roman nobles ; whose high destiny
It was·to clear the way for gospel light,
Through boundless regions of barbaric night ;
Bequeathing the world's empire at his fall,
That all mankind might hear Messiah's call !
Thus, not in vain, fulfilling Heaven's behest,
Did Rome's dominion spread from East to West,
Breaking down barriers of mind and race,
To usher in a reign of Christian grace.

Yes ;—here at Rome, where Jove in glory reigned,
The Christian Cross its earliest triumphs gained ;

Though scorned by Pagans, and baptized in blood,
The faith, once planted, took deep root, and stood
Firm amid persecution's fiercest storms,
When countless gazers marked the bleeding forms
Of martyrs on yon Coliseum's stage,
Nor spared the feebleness of sex or age ;—
Crouching in catacombs, the faith still spread,
Gaining fresh life 'mid galleries of dead ;
Till, struggling through three centuries of night,
Christ's banner waved on the Tarpeian height ;
Rome's Emperor reared the Cross—and all was light!

Henceforth the Church's onward course we trace
Enfolding Europe in her wide embrace;
Princes and people learning to obey,
Alike submissive to her priestly sway.
Firm as a rock exposed to ocean's rage,
She saw the world progress from age to age ;
Saw Error strive in vain to vanquish Truth,
Fresh in the vigour of perpetual youth ;
Saw armies marshalled at her very gate,
Yet quailed not,—rendering only love for hate ;
Believing that Christ's promise could not fail,
" Against my Church no foe shall e'er prevail ! "

PART III.

——◆——

LAYS OF HOME-LAND.

To Woman.

—o—

I

SOURCE of our dearest joys in life !
Maid, mother, sister, friend, or wife,—
   Woman ! be thou my theme !
From man's first state ordained to be
Arbitress of his destiny—
   Bright angel of his dream !

2

Since erst I drew my infant breath
I 've loved thee, and will love till death
   Shall sever the communion ;
And still I 'll hope, when this poor clay
Shall crumble, in glad realms of day
   To recommence the union !

3

Through every shifting scene of life,
'Mid ocean's roar and battle strife,
  My guardian wast thou ever!
In time of peril, sickness, need,
How oft thy prayer did intercede
  To save me,—failing never!

4

Oh! while this vital spark shall linger,
Still may thy faithful warning finger
  Point out the path of duty!
May thy dear arm support my head
In death's last anguish;—thine eye shed
The last fond tear beside my bed;
  Then—farewell Love and Beauty!

A Christmas Carol.

*(On seeing the Morning Star shining brilliantly on
Christmas Morn.)*

—o—

I

How glorious in the eastern sky
Glows yon lone star ! like God's own eye
   O'er dark earth smiling ;
As when, on this auspicious morn,
Angels announced a Saviour born,
   Heaven reconciling !

2

For then, as now, a bright lone star
Was hailed by sages, from afar
   Their footsteps guiding ;
Until o'er Bethlehem it hovered,
And, to their wondering gaze, discovered
   A Babe abiding !

3

Around that Babe there shone a glory ;
While o'er him angels sang the story
   Of God's great love ;
Proclaiming " Peace " to Adam's race,
For all who to the proffered grace
   Submissive prove.

4

Star of the East ! as now we gaze
This morn on thee, oh ! let thy rays
   Our hearts illume
With lasting light of joy and peace,
That may, when life on earth shall cease,
   Survive the tomb !

A New-Year's Greeting.

(To a Young French Lady on New Year's Eve 1871–72.)

—o—

1

DEAR Jeanne ! the old year wanes;
   'Twas born in sorrow,
Amidst a nation's pains,
War's woes and bloody stains ;
But now, Peace once more reigns ;
   Hail, happier morrow !

2

Hail to thee, noble France !
   Thy dark days ended ;
Look up with hopeful glance
To the new year's advance,
No more the sport of chance,
   By Heaven befriended !

3

Hail to thee, maiden sweet !
Life's course beginning ;
Be it thy lot to meet
Friends where'er roam thy feet,
Making thy joys complete,
Fond hearts still winning.

4

But, oh ! keep memory fast
'Mid all thy pleasure !
Think of those in days past
Who, 'mid the tempest blast,
When skies were overcast,
Gave France their leisure ;

5

Striving her wounds to bind
'Mid war's commotion ;
Ne'er to her sorrows blind,
Aided by woman kind,
Each with true heart and mind
Worked with devotion !

6

May France rest evermore,
  Peace still possessing !
Healed be each angry sore !
Long may she Him adore
Who doth to her outpour
  Each truest blessing !

A Birthday Sonnet.

(To a Girl on completing her twenty-first year.)

—◦—

THY life's sweet spring is past! its early flowers,
Once redolent of hope and joy and love,
Droop their sad heads, desponding.   Time doth
    prove
All perishable; childhood's careless hours
Slip by unheeded.   Onward still we move
From infancy to age, but feel the change
Scarce more than trees their growth.   Spring's
    genial showers
Give place to summer's sun ; each hath its range.
Maiden ! *thy* summer's first morn on thee smiles ;
'Tis time youth's crop should ripen ; ay ! and yield
Virtue's choice fruit, unspoilt by vice's wiles.
May guardian spirits be thy guide and shield ;
Thus shall autumnal glories on thee wait,
And winter find thee ready for thy fate !

A Farewell to " May."

(Sent to Miss " May " F., on her departure to India.)

—o—

1

PAUSE yet awhile, old Winter drear!
Restrain thy rapid flight;
For once, I bid thee linger here,
Since with thee one must disappear
Most precious in my sight.

2

Not now, alas! shall smiling spring
Raise gladness in my heart,
Though fresh flowers in its train it bring,
And blithesome birds to chirp and sing;
For oh! 'twill bid me part

3

From her! the fairest flower that blows,
Combining all in one;—
The lily, violet, and rose;
Bearing rich gifts from each, she goes
To regions of the sun.

4

And summer too, though bright and gay,
   Shall strike my heart with chill ;
Its smiles will seem but to betray ;
For what is summer without "May" ?
   Oh, 'tis but winter still !

5

Yet one blest flower the earth shall bear
   On many a lonely spot ;
The sight of it shall oft soothe care,
While from my heart ascends the prayer,
   "Sweet May, Forget-me-not ! "

The Lily of the Vale.

—o—

1

FAIR, modest flower! whose drooping bells
   Sweetest of scents exhale ;
In grove or garden none excels
   The " Lily of the Vale."

2

The elfin queen her court doth hold
   Within thy belfry pale,
And doth to thee her charms unfold,
   Sweet " Lily of the Vale."

3

There nightly she delights to hear
   Some lover's plaintive tale,
Sprinkling with many a dewy tear
   Each " Lily of the Vale."

4

Oh ! that her sympathising aid
She'd proffer, and prevail,
To melt the heart of yon dear maid,
My " Lily of the Vale ! "

The Countess Canning.

(A Sonnet in Memoriam.)

———o———

A NOBLE lady !—Perfect type of all
That men most love and honour in her sex ;
Hers not alone the outward grace that decks
Beauty's fair form our senses to enthral,
But *loveliness of soul*, surviving wrecks
Wherewith Time strews our track. Where duty
    led
Thither she followed ; perils that appal
Men of strong mould blanched not her cheek with
    dread.
India's first Viceroy's wife, she reigned—a queen !
'Mid faction's frowns and dark rebellion's night
Her lord's true star, till day returned serene ;
Proved woman's worth ; then winged her heaven-
    ward flight !

Lo! where she loved to walk by Hooghly's wave,
The grateful Hindoo scatters flowers around her
    grave!*

---

* She was buried in the Government Park at Barrackpore, where a beautiful monument has been erected to her memory, around which daily offerings of flowers are deposited by native visitors.

On Three Graves in Westminster Abbey.

(A Sonnet in Memoriam, written in 1863.)

———o———

CANNING!—CLYDE!—OUTRAM!—Side by side
    they lie
 Neath the vast vault, 'mid England's mighty dead;
A glorious trio!—Struggling at the head
Of empire and of armies, victory
Crowned their joint deeds, by right and valour led
Where rude rebellion reared its blood-stained crest
Stern justice triumphed, linked with clemency;
The land, no more by anarchy oppressed,
Hailed its new Empress; old things passed away;
A bright day dawned o'er India's darkened plain;
Subject no more to lucre's sordid sway,
Her grateful millions greet us o'er the main,
And see, in yon amalgamated dust,
An augury of future harmony and trust.

In Memoriam.

*On the Burial of Field-Marshal Sir George Pollock, G.C.B.,
G.C.S.I., in Westminster Abbey, October 16, 1872.*

—*o*—

ONCE more the Abbey opens its wide portal !
Another Indian hero claims a grave
Beside his compeers !   Through the lofty nave,
Sacred to Britain's sons of fame immortal,
An aged warrior, borne by comrades brave,
Receives the last sad tribute to his worth ;
While solemn words of Holy Writ exhort all
Wisely to use, like him, life's span on earth.
Pollock ! 'twas thine thy country's wound to heal,*
Thine to restore the lustre of her arms ;

---

* Sir George Pollock reconquered Cabul after the disasters of
1841, and brought back the British captives in safety to India.

To teach the foe once more our power to feel,
And snatch our captives back to freedom's charms.
Farewell, old friend ! chief of a gifted race ;
Mourned by the brave and good, we yield thee to
    God's grace !

On the Death of a New-born Infant.

—o—

1

ANGELIC pledge of wedded love,
  Yearned for in hope full long ;
Like a bright vision from above,
  Where holy cherubs throng,
Thou cam'st, a messenger of grace,
With heaven's own glory round thy face.

2

How thrilled our hearts when first thy cry
  Greeted our eager ears !
It seemed an echo from the sky
  To calm our fruitless fears,
And bade us breathe a parent's blessing
Our first-born treasure while possessing.

3

Ah ! who can tell the grateful pride
  That filled the mother's breast,
When, softly breathing, by her side
  Her babe was laid to rest ?

A new light dawned upon her soul,
Her woman's part at length made whole.

4

But brief, alas ! her new-found joy ;
    For while she calmly slumbered,
Death's angel snatched away her boy,
    Its hours of life were numbered !
Its earthly form proved but the portal
Through which to pass to bliss immortal !

5

It lives ! a sinless child of grace ;
    Our treasure's safe in heaven !
It serves the Saviour face to face,
    Free from all earthly leaven :
At such blest lot shall we repine ?
O God ! it was not ours, but Thine !

6

Thine, with the host around Thy throne
    To warble forth Thy praise ;
Ah ! pity us, left here alone,
    Guide us, through Wisdom's ways,
To where loved souls have gone before ;
There not to part for evermore !

Story of a Bird in a Cage, and the Song it Warbled.

—o—

1

THERE lived not long ago in Onslow Square
A maiden as forlorn as she was fair ;
All day disconsolate and dull she sate,
Bewailing ever her unwedded state.

2

Whene'er the bell a visitor announced,
Her fluttering heart within her bosom bounced,
Hoping that in each stranger she'd discover
That rare phenomenon—a real lover!

3

Her father used to scold, and say, " My child !
I never knew a girl like you so wild ;
I really must some dame demure provide,
Who over you shall prudently preside."

4

Whereat, alarmed, she 'd cry in coaxing strain,
"O dear Papa! unsay those words again!
Let me but reign quiescent in this house,
I promise to be quiet as a mouse!"

Song.

Yes, dear Papa! I 'll be so prim,
  So dutiful and prudent,
Don't get me a duenna grim;
  I 'll toil like any student.

Sometimes I 'll sing, and sometimes play
  Upon the grand piano;
And I 'll appoint a special day
  To talk Italiano.

Some happy hours, too, I 'll beguile
  With water-colour brushes;
No gossiper shall gain my smile,
  No booby raise my blushes.

So, dear Papa! do let me but
  This once my own point carry,
My eyes, henceforth, I 'll try to shut
  On all men—till I marry.

But then, Papa ! for my poor sake
   Do quickly try to find
Some handsome fellow, who will make
   A husband to my mind.

I don't want one too thin and long,
   Nor one too fat and short ;
But one who sings a jolly song,
   And can enjoy some sport.

I 'd like him, too, to have some hair
   Upon his lip and chin ;
But whether he be dark or fair
   Don't signify a pin !

You recollect that Mr D.
   Who went last year to Rome ;
Well, that 's the sort of man for me ;
   I wish he would but come !

Then, too, there 's Mr W.,
   Oh ! if he had but popped !
I need not then to trouble you ;
   But off to Ind he 's hopped.

I need not speak of Colonel R.,
  Though he 's so kind a friend ;
For he 's, you know, too old by far,
  So there 's of him an end !

Few other beaux have I to name
  Who round my path have fluttered ;
None ever yet has raised a flame,
  Or word of courtship muttered.

Thus, dear Papa ! you see I 'm free,
  And of my freedom sick !
So bring a husband home to me,
  And oh, Papa !—be QUICK !

To

General Sir Archdale Wilson, G.C.B., the Conqueror of Delhi.

(In Acknowledgment of a fine Salmon caught in the Dee.)

—o—

1

HAIL! great Sir Archdale; thy renown
From Indus to the pole has flown;
   From Delhi to the Dee
The right man thou, beyond a doubt,
To catch a Tartar or a trout,
   By river, lake, or sea!

2

In happy hour thou didst annul
The empire of the Great Mogul;
   The whole world knows the story;
How, undismayed by scorching sun
Or countless hosts, was nobly won
   Thy conqueror's wreath of glory!

3

And now, from war's red fields retired,
Thy breast, with hero's ardour fired,
   Still pants for victory's prizes ;
Triumphant still, with rod and fly
Thou may'st be seen with eager eye,
   Where trout or salmon rises.

4

Still undeterred by storm or toil,
And ready, too, to *share* thy spoil,
   Thy friendship's no mere gammon ;
Long may'st thou live to fight and fish,
Enjoying every earthly wish ;
   And oh, thanks for the salmon !

An Acrostic to the Same.

(*On a similar occasion.*)

—o—

S ALVE ! great captor of big fish ! once more
I welcome a fine salmon at my door ;
R hyming rude thanks from homely Muse's store.

A h ! oft, I ween, by side of " Bonnie Dee,"
R eclining on its bank with rod in hand,
C ontemplative, thy spirit, soaring free,
H ies to the scenes where Delhi's soldier band
D id deeds of might, destined to live in story,
A nd crowned their chief with victory's proud bays ;
L ong may he live, their monument of glory,
E nding in blest tranquillity his days !

W ell done, brave fisherman ! not all in vain
I n life's wide waters thou hast cast thy fly ;
L et Jumna's gory stream attest thy gain,
S preading the tidings of thy victory
O nward to immortality's vast ocean !
N ow, dear Sir A. ! accept my heart's devotion !

Echoes of a London Season.

THE echoes of a London season
Furnish for rhyme a fitting reason ;
What stirring visions they recall
Of rout and opera and ball !
Of flower shows, fancy fairs, flirtations,
Exciting blissful palpitations ;
Of noonday rides in Rotten Row,
Where each belle finds her favourite beau,
To follow up his last night's banter
With soft confessions—at a canter !
While fond Papa, politely blind,
Lags, at a trot, not far behind,
Discussing politics and horses,
Seasoned with scandal and divorces.

Yes !—For a fashionable miss
London supplies supremest bliss ;

She loves a suffocating squeeze
Far better than the seaside breeze;
Prefers the cabman's ceaseless rattle
To birds' sweet songs, or bleat of cattle;
A bonnet shop to beds of flowers;
"Howell and James" to Eden's bowers!

On Sunday she selects as teacher
Some popular sensation preacher;
And deems it dutiful and meet
To work choice slippers for his feet,
Thus consecrating Sabbath leisure
By holy act of pious pleasure.
Fit mate for such bewitching belle
Is the true fashionable "swell;"
'Twould baffle my descriptive powers
To tell how *he* fills up his hours;
What with cheroots, clubs, calls, Cremorne,
He dawdles through the day forlorn,
Still voting everything "a bore,"
Yet longing still for something more.

For men who thus their moments trifle,
What a rare godsend is the rifle!

Hail ! Wimbledon ! whose tented plain
Lies within easy reach by train ;
Long be it thine our youth to lure
To manly sports and pastimes pure ;
To fire their hearts with patriot's flame ;
To train their hands to perfect aim ;
To qualify them for the fight
Against our foes' invading might ;
To make them self-reliant, calm,
With earnest heart and steady arm ;
Staunch sons of Freedom's sacred sod,
True to their country and their God !

Somebody's Eyes.

—o—

1

THERE lives a lady in this city
  More beautiful than wise,
And, sad to say, although so pretty,
  She has most wicked eyes.

2

Each unsophisticated beau
  She loves to tantalise,
Till he discovers, to his woe,
  The danger of her eyes.

3

Poor married men she ogles, too,
  And to entice them tries;
Till soon, alas! they learn to rue
  The mischief of her eyes.

4
My stairs descending, oft unseen,
　　I hear her merry cries,
And catch a glimpse behind the screen
　　At those bewitching eyes.

5
All day they haunt me at my work,
　　Though I my thoughts disguise ;
Would that her husband were a Turk !
　　He 'd soon poke out her eyes.

6
But he who owns this frisky fair
　　In vain implores and sighs ;
She laughs at all his anxious care,
　　And rolls about her eyes.

7
Now were this pretty tyrant mine,
　　Regardless of her cries,
I 'd bind her fast with silken twine,
　　And bung up both her eyes.

8
Nor should she taste of meat or drink,
　　Nor from her seat arise,
Until she vowed no more to wink
　　With those most wicked eyes !

A Caution for Somebody.

—o—

1

YOU say I'm "jealous;" but I swear
Your taunt is most unjust;
'Twould be dishonour to the fair
To show such want of trust.

2

Yes, jealousy's a thing I *scorn;*
Besides, 'tis out of fashion;
Oh! better ne'er to have been born
Than yield to such a passion.

3

The jealous man is on a par
With murderers, like Othello;
'Tis surely going much too far
To say I'm like that fellow!

4

But still, I hate to see you dance
    With that young saucy knave ;
Next time he makes his bold advance,
    Pray, mind how you behave !

5

Not that I 'm "jealous," oh ! dear, no !
    But still I cannot bear
To see you go on flirting so ;
    So, prythee, ma'am, beware !

6

Those dancing puppies are a *pest*,
    And ladies of propriety
Should banish each such dangerous guest
    From their discreet society.

7

Therefore, though I 'm most meek and mild,
    And "jealousy" despise,
I caution you to be less wild,
    If you 'd preserve your eyes !

8

It is not "jealousy," but *love*
    That doth these lines provoke ;
And should you disobedient prove,
    By Jove ! 'twill be no joke !

A Valentine.

From Chang, the Chinese Giant, to a very tall young Lady.

—o—

1

STUPENDOUS Miss! thy lofty fame
　　Has reached my longing ear,
Since from Celestial realms I came
In search of one to share my name
　　And be my own true dear.

2

From the first moment of my birth
　　I 've heard that English girls
Excel all others on the earth
For beauty, tenderness, and worth,
　　And wear most lovely curls.

3

So when I grew to man's estate,
　　I forthwith crossed the seas,
Hoping to find, in maiden state,
One tall enough to be my mate,
　　And reach my lips with ease.

4

Your height, I hear, is six feet six,
    While seven feet eight 's my measure ;
If in the way no hindrance sticks
Our wedding-day we soon may fix,
    And take our fill of pleasure.

5

You only need reply " *Chin, chin !* "
    In Pekin's polished slang,
Which means " *I'm thine through thick and thin !* "
Thenceforth our wedlock will begin,
    And I'm thine own true CHANG.

A Valentine from Blue-Beard.

—o—

YOUNG woman ! I 'm a handsome man,
　My beard is long and blue ;
My figure ladies love to scan,
　My heart is warm and true.

That heart I offer now to thee !
　Of course you can't refuse ;
A score at least bleed now for me,
　But you alone I choose.

At the same time, you 'd best *beware*,
　Nor think with me to trifle ;
When my blood 's up I 'm apt to swear,
　And use my sword or rifle !

I 've often married been before,
　As you perhaps have heard ;
Of pickled heads I 've got a score,
　My vengeance who incurred.

Not that I would, for worlds, alarm
  My own sweet " Lovey-dovey,"
Though really, I don't see much harm
  In shooting a whole covey.

But as for *thee*, why should you dread ?
  I love you as myself !
Should I, by chance, cut off your head,
  I 'd place it on a shelf,

And smother it in purest honey
  In token of my sorrow ;
And, in respect for matrimony,
  Marry again to-morrow !

So, lovely maiden, quick decide !
  Nor keep me too long waiting ;
Come, let me hail thee as my bride ;
  My heart is palpitating.

Valentine for Mr Onslow,

Governor of the Wandsworth House of Correction.

—o—

I

ON-SLOW, yet sure, each circling year
    Marches its destined course ;
The green leaves come and disappear,
Stern Winter bringing up the rear
    Upon his pale white horse.

2

On-slow, and ever slowly on,
    Moves yonder prison clock ;
While counting each dull hour that 's gone,
Each prisoner in his cell alone
    Curses the crowing cock.

3

For what cares he that night has fled,
    Since day brings nought but woe ?
No sooner is he out of bed
Than a mask covers up his head,
    And he must move *on-slow !*

4

" *On-slow*, On-slow," is still the word
  That's uppermost with him ;
His cell doth nothing *fast* afford,
Except the door bolt and the cord
  That binds each culprit's limb.

5

And long may bad men get *On-slow*,
  And " fast " men be made fast !
The greatest Governor I know
Is he who keeps his subjects so ;
At Wandsworth he presides, I trow ;
  Long may his empire last !

The Summons of Love.

—o—

1

SUMMONED by love's sweet call, she flew,
  True faith her woman's heart sustaining ;
Old friends fast fading from her view,
With hope she turned to regions new,
  Yet oh! how tedious in attaining!

2

Afar she saw a beckoning hand
  In her life's dream, and one dear voice
Seemed to announce, in accents bland,
A welcome to yon eastern land,
  Bidding her evermore rejoice.

3

But yet, I ween, she struggled sore
  Thus to leave each familiar face
And spot embalmed in memory's store,
Half the wide world to wander o'er
  E'er she should find a resting-place.

4

But harder still to leave behind
 That sacred sod, where oft she wept
O'er one, the gentlest of her kind,
Scarce twelve sad months to Heav'n resigned,
 For there an angel-*mother* slept !

5

But He whose blessing still attends
 A faithful daughter's fond devotion,
Who mercy with affliction blends,
And to the mourner comfort sends,
 Guided her safe across the ocean.

6

Lo ! a hand waves from shore.   'Tis *his !*
 Soon to press hers in gladdening grasp ;
Thenceforth she feels her own it is,
And full once more her cup of bliss
 As to his heart he her doth clasp !

7

Welcome ! thrice welcome, cousin ! wife !
 Beloved so long, though gained so late ;
No more to part again in life,
We 'll brave together this world's strife,
 And love shall ever guard our gate !

.   .   .   .   .

8

A year has passed—and, watchful still,
   Love at his post unwearied stands ;
Long may he thus his part fulfil ;
Nor age nor custom serve to chill
   The flame once lit by Heaven's commands!

To a Young Girl on her Confirmation.

—o—

I

BEHOLD, attired in robes of bridal white,
A youthful maiden reverently kneels;
Angels look down from blest abodes of light,
While she, with upward glance, to Heaven appeals,
The inward struggles of her heart reveals,
To worldly pomps and follies bids adieu,
And her baptismal vows doth solemnly renew.

2

Bending o'er her fair form with outstretched hands,
The mitred priest a blessing doth invoke,
That she, obeying ever God's commands
Which He to Israel's host from Sinai spoke,
May ne'er His mercy slight nor wrath provoke;
Defended by His mighty power and grace,
Till privileged in heaven to see Him face to face!

3

Oh ! who that guileless maiden's face can view
And harbour thought profane within his heart ?
There all that 's pure and innocent and true
Is pictured by fond nature's limning art ;
And better far 'twould be from life to part
Than utter aught, save words of honest truth,
To her who thus to God doth consecrate her youth.

4

Then trust me still, sweet maid ! nor deem me
    dead
To pure religion's soul-subduing sway,
Though oft, by pleasure or by passion led,
I wander far from Wisdom's peaceful way ;
And, when for erring mortals you shall pray,
Oh ! sometimes cast a kindly look on one
Whose path in life hath oft been wearisome and
    lone !

On a Lock of Hair.

—o—

1

AND can it be that the fair girlish head
Where late this ringlet grew in beauty's pride
Now lies unconscious in the grave's cold bed ?
But yesterday we hailed her as a bride,
Full of young life and hope, her chosen swain be-
　　side !
Oh ! could not Death its hand in pity stay,
Or 'midst the aged and wretched find its prey ?

2

Methinks I see her from the altar moving,
Eight ministering maidens in her train ;
Whilst friendly voices, faltering and loving,
Greet her with blessings from all sides ;—in vain !
Few, few, alas ! shall greet that lovely form again :
Not here on earth her destined scene of joy ;
But 'mid God's angels, free from sin's alloy !

3

She 's gone ! and nought left save this lock of hair
To tell of all her living charms and grace !
Dear undecaying relic ! fresh and fair
As when it still adorned her smiling face ;
In this a pledge of immortality we trace :
Reanimate in beauty from the tomb,
Our " Constance " shall arise in Paradise to bloom !

A Birthday Sermon.

——o——

DEAR MARY! if I rightly judge, you will be
 seventeen
About the time this reaches you ; an age still young
 and green ;
The sweetest stage of maidenhood, when yet the
 heart is pure,
Untainted by the follies which betray while they
 allure ;
When all within is love and peace, and hope stands
 at the door
Expectantly, with outstretched wings, inviting you
 to soar,
And scan awhile life's busy scenes, and roam the
 wide wide world,
And bask in Pleasure's beams where her gay banner waves unfurled ;

And all seems good and glorious, as when the
  earth was young,
Ere yet the Serpent had beguiled the woman with
  his tongue.
And now, as then, before thee stand two trees from
  which to choose :
Behold ! my child, the tree of life, which thou
  mayest freely use ;
'Twas planted for thee by God's Son ; 'twas watered
  with his blood ;
And, if thou wouldst to bliss attain, be this thy
  daily food.
That *other* tree is also there, whose fruit is still forbidden ;
More fair and tempting to the eye, but inwardly lies
  hidden
That deadly poison known as SIN—oh ! fear of it
  to taste !
Oh ! harbour not so foul a fiend within thy bosom
  chaste !
So shall thy path through life be safe, though storms
  may rage around ;
So shall thy soul, when life is past, in God's own
  fold be found.

  .   .   .   .   .

And now, farewell, dear girl! be thine to choose
the better part;
To shun what God forbids, and yield to Him thy
youthful heart;
To take the fruit He offers thee, though less sweet
it may seem
Than that which grows in Guilt's parterre beside
her poisonous stream.
Blest be thy future lot in life, cloudless thy calm career,
Whether in maiden's bower to bide, or bound by
ties more dear!
And still a cherished corner keep within thy
woman's breast
For him whose *home** is in the East, whose *heart* is
in the West :
Who daily bids the sun's beams kiss thy lips ere he
decline,
And bring, with morn's returning rays, a token too
from thine :
Whose love, like electricity, doth round the earth
extend;
Whose pen once more records " Farewell ! "—thy
father and thy friend.

---

* This was written from India to a girl in England.

On a Marriage in Westminster Abbey.

(Wednesday, July 14, 1869.)

1

BEHOLD ! in wedding garb arrayed,
A noble youth and lovely maid,
    Earth's choicest gifts possessing,
Before the sacred altar stand,
Hand reverently joined in hand,
    To seek the Church's blessing.

2

Behind them grouped, in virgin gear,
Nine young attendant nymphs appear,
    Bright gems of British beauty !
Whilst the vast sympathising throng
Responsive join in choral song,
    To aid love's crowning duty.

3

There too, obeying friendship's call,
Are seen the noblest pair of all*
In England's empire ample ;
Happy themselves in mutual love,
Long in sweet wedlock may they prove
A bright and blest example !

4

And hark ! a voice as soft as honey†
Utters the spell of matrimony !
Insidiously stealing
Into lone hearts, it stirs to life
Fond longings for a loving wife,
To home-born joys appealing.

5

Those venerable aisles, I ween,
Have witnessed many a wondrous scene
In history's page recorded ;
Yet none more notably than this
Exemplifying human bliss
Have ages past afforded.

. . . . .

---

* The Prince and Princess of Wales honoured the ceremony with their royal presence.
† Bishop Wilberforce performed the service.

6

The irrevocable words are spoken !
The bride's hand wears the golden token !
 Two hearts now blend in one !
None shall that holy bond dissever,
Destined, we trust, to last for ever,
 Thus hopefully begun !

To an Elderly Lady.

ON MY DEPARTURE FOR EGYPT.

Brindisi, Dec. 1st, 1872.

—⁂—

1

DEAR LADY !—(may I call you "dear" ?)—
  Since that sad day in Welchpool town,
When to your window you drew near
And seemed to drop a farewell tear,
  My heart has been with grief bowed down !

2

Silent since then I 've borne that sore ;
  But now, from Europe's strand departing,
Bound for drear Afric's desert shore,
I send to her whom I adore
  These lines from Brindisi ere starting.

3

Farewell ! but ever of thee thinking,
  Waking or dreaming ; whether floating

O'er ocean's depths, or in them sinking,
Oblivion's waters never drinking ;
 In life, in death, on thee I 'm doting !

4

Or when, from top of pyramid,
 I see old Nile beneath me flowing,
Below whose golden sands lie hid
Secrets of which the world 's well rid,
 Still in my heart a flame is glowing ;

5

And should you covet some last token
 When I become a tongueless dummy,
Reminding you of fond words spoken,
And loving vows in life ne'er broken,
 Say—*would you like a little mummy ?*

6.

If so, I 'll ransack when at Cairo,
 At Thebes, and every other place,
The tombs of all the race of Pharaoh,
Until one fitting I lay bare, oh !
 May it recall to thee my face !

To a Pair of Twin Sisters.

(From Venice, Nov. 1872.)

—o—

DEAR GEMINI !—Papa and I
    With all the fire of youth
Have had a spree from sea to sea,
    Yea, right from North to South !
At Paris first he on us burst
    Just like a clap of thunder ;
Each from our cup jumped nimbly up
    And greeted him with wonder.
For three whole days, filled with amaze,
    We rushed about quite frantic,
No shop or church escaped our search
    Amid our walks romantic.
At Versailles grand, a Countess bland
    To lunch our party greeted ;
Thence to the hall, where statesmen all
    We saw in hundreds seated.
Their President, on business bent,
    In vain his bell oft sounded ;

The noise and gabble of that queer rabble
 Our senses quite confounded.
Of the mad class of RABAGAS *
 We saw full many a sample ;
Of rulers such we don't think much,
 If these be an example !
Next, off by train, Italia's plain
 We reached in wondrous hurry,
Through tunnel dashing without a smashing,
 Or the least bit of flurry.
Ere leaving France we caught a glance
 Of light from the sun's quiver,
But in Italy, oh ! we found deep snow,
 And felt inclined to shiver.
At Turin one day we kept Sunday,
 And rambled through the city ;
At all he saw, your dad's wise jaw
 Pronounced it " nice " and " pretty."
To Venice fast we came at last,
 That city built in ocean ;
In gondolas gay gliding all day,
 The luxury of motion !

---

* RABAGAS is the famous hero of the popular comedy so named,
wherein the democrats of Paris were held up to ridicule.

'Mid noble halls we made our calls,
   Where DOGES lived in splendour,
Then after dark, in SQUARE ST MARK,
   Ourselves to ease surrender.
Alas ! to-morrow, to our sorrow,
   We destined are to part ;
To Egypt we, to Naples he,
   So, good-bye, each sweetheart !

A Red Cross Acrostic.

—o—

[Dedicated to "La Société Nationale Anglaise de Secours, aux
Malades et Blessés Militaires," as a souvenir of their work
in "Les Anciennes Casernes," at Boulogne-sur-Mer, from
August 1870 to May 1872.

" L OVE ONE ANOTHER!"   Such was the command
E xpressed by Jesus to His chosen band,
S oon to be scattered over every land.

A las!   Since then, long centuries have past,
N or quite forgotten is that farewell voice! [blast
C hrist's faith has spread afar ; but WAR'S dread
I s heard too oft !—Not yet may Earth rejoice
E mancipated from her bonds of evil ;
N ot yet is chained her ancient foe—the Devil ;
N or has her prophesied "Millennium" come ;
E xcited millions march to beat of drum ;
S till—LOVE'S angelic tones are heard amid
    the hum !

"C HARITY NEVER FAILS ! "—Oh, blessed truth !
A ttested by kind deeds in every age ;
S trong in the ardour of eternal youth,
E arning fresh triumphs over man's mad rage !
R eceive this tribute from the few staunch friends
N ow ceasing their joint labours in thy cause !
E ternal be the PEACE their work which ends !
S oon may LOVE reign on earth, and all obey
    its laws !

The True and Wonderful History of the Dog Dandy.

By his own Master.

— o —

THIS is the veracious history of a veritable Dog. Each Canto describes a distinct epoch of his existence, and every incident is based upon some fact of his canine experience.

The history of his wife "Flora" is also embodied. They were SPANIEL SETTERS of thoroughbred parents ; and their joint adventures have been thus appropriately celebrated in purest DOG-REL, by special desire, to accompany a genuine portrait of "Dandy," which was painted by a talented lady artist and admirer for a recent Fine Art Exhibition at Bombay.

Dandy's military career, like that of other distinguished heroes, such as Wellington and Napoleon, was so closely interwoven with the history of his country, that a few brief introductory memoranda may be necessary for the better understanding of the first Canto, relating to his "Campaign in Oude."

This occurred in 1857–58, when the Indian Mutiny and its attendant struggles found full occupation for the small handful of British troops available for its suppression. The story opens at that most critical period when the two great capitals of Delhi and Lucknow were in possession of formidable hosts of mutineers and insurgents; when Generals Neil and Havelock were struggling against the ferocious Nana near Cawnpore, and making heroic efforts to reach the Lucknow Residency, where the brave Henry Lawrence still protected hundreds of English-women and children against a countless multitude of armed besiegers, with the aid of a weak and half-starved garrison of his countrymen; while his brother officer of the Bengal Artillery, Archdale Wilson, held in check several thousands of disciplined sepoys who had concentrated within the walls of Delhi, to stake their lives upon one great struggle for the Empire of India.

Such was the momentous crisis of affairs, when "Dandy" took the field, and, perhaps, turned the scales in favour of the English. His subsequent adventures scarcely need explanation.

They are now reprinted, by permission, from Routledge's *Boy's Magazine.*

CANTO THE FIRST.

HIS CAMPAIGN IN OUDE.

I

"DANDY," whose portrait here you see,
Was born of purest pedigree,
While travelling to Bengal by sea.

2

" FLORA," his sister, friend, and wife,
Sprang simultaneously to life,
Nor once exchanged they words of strife.

3

No sooner in Calcutta landed,
Than off to Oude they were commanded,
Where foes were mutinously banded.

4

Though early thus to war inured,
To crime they never were allured,
Nor were their canine lives insured.

5

Ah! 'twas a fray that tried the mettle
Of dogs and men!—more hard to settle
Than contest betwixt Pot and Kettle.

6

'Gainst fearful odds, 'neath scorching sun,
Brave Neil and Havelock fought and won,
And yet their task seemed scarce begun.

7

For, still hemmed round by traitor host,
Lawrence stood firm at peril's post—
Of Indian heroes honoured most!

8

And still, on Delhi's parching plain,
Wilson's staunch warriors strove in vain
Yon rebel citadel to gain.

9

But lo ! with Persian laurels crowned,
Outram obeys the trumpet's sound,
" Aye ready " where most blows abound.

10

Havelock—Neil—Outram—blest alliance
Wherewith to bid the foe defiance,
Nerving all hearts with fresh reliance.

11

E'en Dandy wagged his puppy tail,
Eager the rebels to assail,
While Flora howled a warlike wail.

12

Onward ! resistless as a wave
Our soldiers swept, resolved to save
Their comrades from a cruel grave:

13

Backward ! from Cawnpore to Lucknow
The foe were driven—to them, I trow,
Foretaste of final overthrow.

14

The city reached, warm waxed the fight
From street to street, till, welcome sight !
The baffled traitors took to flight.

15

Dandy and Flora in the rear,
With loud " bow-wows " contrived to clear
Their way through foemen venturing near.

16

The gate was neared ! Soon hand grasped
    hand
Of each devoted soldier-band ;
Some strong men wept—for once unmanned.

DANDY IN OUDE.—*Page* 178.

17

Still, hampered with some scores of sick,
Wounded and women scattered thick,
'Twas plain that there the force must stick

18

Till reinforcements should arrive;
And Dandy meanwhile must contrive
To keep himself and spouse alive.

19

Two months in garrison cooped up,
With empty dish and cheerless cup,
They seldom found whereon to sup;

20

And famished soldiers oft would flurry
Their minds, by hinting how much worry
'Twould save—to cook of them a curry!

21

But though reduced to skin and bone,
They still retained their valiant tone,
·Nor ever joined in croaker's groan.

22

In very nick of time at last
Clyde came to terminate their fast,
And o'er their gloom a light to cast !

23

Thus was Lucknow twice sought and saved ;
Thus Dandy and his wife both braved
The fight ! and gallantly behaved !

24

Not e'en the Generals who led all,
Better deserved the Lucknow medal
Than these brave doggies :—Now I've said all

25

That 's known for certain on the matter,
Till great guns came Lucknow to batter,
By which time Dandy had got fatter ;

26

In fact, had grown to dog's estate,
With Flora for his fitting mate :—
His next adventures I 'll relate.

CANTO THE SECOND.

DANDY'S MARRIED LIFE IN BENGAL.

27

FULL six months more of Oude campaign,
Marching here, there, and back again,
Failed to lay " Dandy" with the slain.

28

Though oft the bullets o'er him flew,
Their aim proved happily untrue,
Or he'd have ne'er been known to you.

29

Flora passed likewise free from harm
Through every danger and alarm,
Increasing daily in each charm.

30

At length, when war's rude deeds were done,
Laden with laurels fairly won,
Dandy and Flora longed for fun.

31

Removed to Ishapore's green glades,*
They roamed at large 'mid rural shades,
The pets of matrons, men, and maids ;

32

Or, romping ever side by side,
They plunged in Hoogly's rapid tide,
And greedy crocodiles defied.

33

But chiefly 'twas their joint delight
To chase a duck, till, mad with fright,
It quacked, then dived quite out of sight.

34

Perplexed, they wildly gazed about,
Till ducky's head afar popped out,
Then recommenced the race and rout.

* A beautiful official residence near Calcutta, where Dandy's master filled an important appointment under Government.

35

Like two attendant satellites,
They shared with us each day's delights,
And guarded our repose by nights.

36

Oh! happiest days of doggish life!
To me with pleasant memories rife,
Remote from worldly care and strife.

37

Five tranquil years thus slid along,
Like the sweet cadence of a song,
When lo! once more the world's loud throng!

38

Farewell! calm shades of Ishapore,
Which we have rambled o'er and o'er!
We ne'er, alas! may see you more!

39

Yet do you ever present seem—
Our never-tiring fireside theme;
Most real once, though now a dream!

40

Linked with those scenes, what visions rise
Of friends whose love we used to prize ;
Some gone before us to the skies !

41

Alas for Flora !—Dandy's mate—
We mourn her cruel tragic fate,
Cut off by bullet in her pate.

42

I draw a curtain o'er the reason
Assigned for that dark act of treason,—
Which happened in the " Dog-day " season.

43

To India, too, a fond farewell !
Where long it was my lot to dwell,
As best the " Army List " can tell.

44

I owe thee much, though doomed to grub
In gloom full fifteen years a " sub,"
Like grim Diogenes in tub.

45

Though oft thy heat half drove me mad,
And I felt weary, sick, and sad,
Still 'twere unjust to call thee bad.

46

Thou first didst offer a career
And goal towards which my youth might steer,
Without which life had been more drear.

47

In thee, too, I found all that tends
To man's chief happiness, and ends
With that best good which Heaven sends.

48

Therefore, to thee my thanks are due,
India ! though faded now from view—
Long may'st thou find good men and true !

CANTO THE THIRD.

DANDY A WIDOWER IN ENGLAND.

49

BEHOLD us, then, returned once more
To our own native English shore,
Old "Dandy" with us, as of yore.

50

We left him in Bengal behind,
But could not reconcile the mind
To separation so unkind.

51

So soon he followed in a ship,
After we gave him thus the slip,
And seemed much better for the trip.

52

The captain and his sailor crew
Wept loud while bidding him adieu,
Waving their hands till hid from view.

53

Coaching through London's crowded street,
The Prince and Princess,* as was meet,
Came forth in chaise to gaze and greet.

54

Dandy, with tail in constant motion,
Expressed his loyal heart's devotion,
Giving of his high breed a notion.

55

Astonished much at all he saw,
He eloquently waved his paw,
While loud " bow-wows " employed his jaw.

56

But soon, with love of freedom fired,
Of a town pent-up life he tired,
And to some country sport aspired.

---

* This actually occurred while Dandy was *en route* from the docks
to the west-end of London.

57

Accepting a friend's invitation,
He started from a railway station,
And was received with loud ovation.

58

Four lovely human sister graces
Rushed to the door with frantic faces,
And smothered him with fond embraces.

59

While their four brothers, one in mind,
Seized each a paw in struggle kind ;
Two pulled before and two behind.

60

Dandy, enraptured with each kiss,
Thought, "*If there be a bower of bliss
For dogs on earth, oh ! it is this !*"

61

Right merrily time now flew past ;
But soon the sky grew overcast,—
Such pleasure was too great to last.

DANDY IN ENGLAND.—*Page* 189.

62

Whether by instinct or by reason,
Dandy divined 'twas shooting season,
Nor deemed a day's sport could be treason :

63

For he was neither knave nor fool,
But had been bred in freedom's school,
Where " game-laws " exercise no rule.

64

One day they walked him off to cricket ;
But while the boys played " single wicket,"
He cast an eye on yonder thicket ;

65

And, lolling waggishly his tongue,
Said to himself, " Now, I 'll be hung
If I 'm not soon those trees among ! "

66

No sooner said than done, egad !
Off to the woods he dashed like mad,
And after him strode each stout lad.

67

But soon, alas ! his pleasure ended ;
For, sniffing where the *pheasants* wended,
He had been shot unless befriended.

68

Keepers, enraged at loss of game,
Dandy a " poaching thief " proclaim,
Giving him thus an evil name.

69

So back he hurried straight to town,
With his tail drooping sadly down,
And on his noble face—a frown !

70

That night he groaned aloud in sleep ;
His thoughts were far beyond the deep
Where Flora lay—'mid mouldering heap.

71

To dissipate his melancholy,
He tried a round of London folly ;
But vain the effort to be jolly.

72

Though free o'er Rotten Row to range,
All seemed insipid, stale, and strange :
The doctors recommended change.

CANTO THE FOURTH.

DANDY A PILGRIM TO ROME.

73

HAVING got somewhat tired of home,
We started off forthwith to Rome,
And visited St Peter's dome.

74

For Dandy, in dejection sunk,
And feeling some religious funk,
Had half a mind to be a monk ;

75

And inwardly made resolution,
That, ere the sun's next revolution,
He'd seek the Church's absolution.

76

While passing convents, without fail
He vehemently wagged his tail,
Showing his wish to *take the veil.*

77

His widowed heart sighed for poor Flora,
So many years her staunch adorer,
And oft he prayed *Pro nobis ora !*

78

Such was his sanctimonious turn
That Latin prayers he tried to learn,
Seated in church sedate and stern.

79

And when the priests would lowly *bow,*
He grumbled forth a smothered *wow,*
An edifying fact, I trow !

80

Losing him at the Coliseum,
Lo! in the Lateran Museum
I found him barking a "Te Deum."

81

Where'er we went, he took his place
On carriage-box, and thus his face
Was known to all the Roman race.

82

The Pope deemed him so prepossessing,
That once he paused, while men addressing,
To give this dog his special blessing.*

83

A famous sculptor, named Benzoni,
So loved him that, one day, alone he
Modelled in clay his canine crony.

84

In fact, were I to mention all
That did this wondrous dog befall,
Folk might me a " romancer " call.

---

* On St Anthony's Day at Rome it is customary to bring animals
from the neighbouring " Campagna " for the Pope's blessing.

85

Naples and the Pompeian Forum
He visited with due decorum,
And saw Vesuvius smoking o'er 'em.

86

Thence to the famous isle of Ischia,
Whose wine, though not so strong as whisky, a
Dose of it soon made Dandy friskier.

87

By Genoa, Milan, and the lakes
His route the homeward traveller takes
Ere he Italian land forsakes.

88

In Como's water, for a spree,
He plunged and swam about with glee,
Right glad to find himself so free.

89

Thence o'er the Alps to bright Lucerne,
He saw each place of note by turn,
Ere summer's sun had ceased to burn.

90

To Paris last at length he came,
Nor deem him very much to blame
If he pronounced it dull and tame ;

91

For was it not an insult great,
Enough to rouse his lasting hate,
To thrust a *muzzle* o'er his pate ?

92

Nevertheless, he was not blind
To those famed charms of form and mind
Which are in " Eugenie " combined,

93

And, spite of ignominious gag,
Whene'er *she* passed his tail would mag-
Nanimously begin to wag.

94

But her imperial lord with scowl
He greeted, muttering a growl,
Which culminated in a howl.

95

For be he dog or be he man,
No freeborn British subject can
Submit to foreign tyrant's ban.

96

And Dandy's soul in wrath would revel
To find himself put on a level
With poodle, pug, and printer's devil!

97

To Calais having paid his fare,
Behold him next in easy-chair
Smoking his pipe with lordly air.

98

Settled in cozy kitchen nook,
He hinted lately to the cook
His purpose soon to *write a book*.

99

Meanwhile this rude sketch I indite,
Lest death should dog and master smite,
And Dandy be forgotten quite.

DANDY AN AUTHOR.—*Page* 196.

100

'Tis fit, ere ending, I should mention
Her Majesty's benign intention
To grant him a " good-service pension ; "

101

And therewith on him to bestow
The post—ne'er held by dog till now—
Of " HONORARY BOW-WOW-WOW ! "

.   .   .   .   .   .

Kind friends, farewell !   May you as safely
　　steer
Your course through life, and work out a career
As good as that you find recorded here.

> DANDY'S mortal career closed on 15th
> March 1872, in his sixteenth year.   His
> cocked-hat and pipe are carefully preserved
> until claimed for the Kensington Museum.

PART IV.

———◆———

LAYS OF RHINE-LAND.

The Hindoo Maiden.

(Suggested by a little prose tale in Andersen's "Bilderbuch ohne Bilder.")

—o—

1

WHERE rolls the Ganges' sacred flood
Through forests dense, lo! from a wood
    Stept a young Hindoo maid;
Slim as a fawn and full of grace,
As beautiful as Eve her face,
    In Nature's charms arrayed.

2

Her open countenance revealed
The thoughts her loving heart concealed;
    Whilst tripping o'er the ground,
Her sandalled feet the wild thorns grazed,
The startled game rushed out amazed
    From their night haunts around.

3

The moon shone bright ; down to the strand
The maiden hastened ; in her hand
    A little lamp she tended ;
Her flushing fingers screened with care
The flickering flame from breath of air,
    As towards the stream she wended.

4

The bank she reached ; the turbid flood
Rushed past, as though in angry mood ;
    The maid turned pale with fear !
" O holy goddess ! shield for me
The flame I now commit to thee ;
    Ah ! save my lover dear ! "

5

Nerved by the prayer, she felt more brave ;
She launched her lamp upon the wave ;
    The current seized its prey !
Anxious, she watched the feeble light,
Now flaring up—now lost to sight,
    Upon its dubious way.

6

Long rooted stood that maiden dark, .
Watching that little floating spark
    With soul-absorbing glance,
Her lustrous eyes, like bright gems beaming,
Through their long silken fringes gleaming,
    As one in waking trance:

7

For, oh! if yon frail lamp burn bright
Until its course be lost to sight,
    Her absent lover lives;
But if by hapless fate extinguished,
Then be her fondest hopes relinquished;
    Gone then each joy life gives.

8

She watched and prayed, with hands fast
    clasped,
Till from her sight the lamp had lapsed;
    A snake slid by unheeded!
With joyous heart her eyes she raised
And the protecting goddess praised;
    " He lives!"—her prayer has speeded.

The Archer.

(Schiller.)

Bow and arrow bearing
  Over hill and dale,
Lo ! the archer daring
  Early day doth hail.

Like the eagle he
  A true monarch is,
Ruling regions free,
  Mountain and abyss.

Far as arrow sweeps
  O'er earth, water, air,
All that flies or creeps
  Is his booty fair.

"*Sleep on, my Heart, in Peace.*"

(From the German.—Rudert.)

——o——

SLEEP on, my heart, in peace !
Night bids all troubles cease,
Distilling dewy showers
On drooping lids of flowers.

Sleep on ! in peace reposing,
Earth's latent life is dozing ;
The moon doth silent shine
Like sentinel divine !

Sleep on ! devoid of fear
Or grief ; for He is near
Who made these worlds so bright,
And keeps all hearts in sight.

Sleep on!—nor let thy rest
By bad dreams be opprest;
In thy faith strongly clad,
Hope o'er thee shining glad!

Sleep on! and should thy breath
Be snatched away by death
'Mid the still hours of night,
Wake thou in realms of light!

Winter.

(From Krummacher.)

—o—

1

HOW calmly dost thou rest,
Clad in thy snowy vest,
   Oh! thou dear Mother-land!
Where now thy songs of spring
From birds of painted wing?
   And flowery festal band?

2

Unclad thou now dost sleep;
No little lambs or sheep
   Upon thy pastures feeding;
The singing birds are dumb,
The bees no longer hum,
   Still, thou art fair exceeding!

3

The twigs and branches shine
With glittering lights divine,
    The eye descries a host !
Say, who hath made thy bed ?
Thy coverlet who spread ?
    And jewelled robe of frost ?

4

The God who reigns above
That wintry garb hath wove,
    He slumbers not nor sleepeth !
Calmly then slumber take
Till he shall bid thee wake,
    And new life o'er thee creepeth.

5

Soon shall returning spring
Its welcome treasures bring
    And renovated powers ;
Where'er its breath shall light,
Earth shall again shine bright
    With garlands of gay flowers !

" The Fall of the Leaf."

(An Autumnal Song.—Von Hoffman.)

—o—

1

FAST now each branch is losing
    Its leaves from tree and bush ;
The sad world seems reposing
    In the grave's silent hush.
Ah! whither have you roved,
Ye little birds beloved ?
    But now so blithely singing !
The frost your foe has proved ;
    Far from us you are winging !

2

Each rock and hedge seems drear,
    In melancholy clad ;
Longer the nights appear,
    The days more short and sad.

Gone are the songsters now
From these dark realms of snow,
    Elsewhere to seek the light;
There once again, I trow,
    They revel in delight.

3

And, when like one that weeps,
    Leaves drop from tree and bush,
And mourning nature sleeps
    In the grave's silent hush;
Shall *we* too droop and sigh?
Ah! no; within thee try
    Perpetual spring to nourish,
So shalt thou care defy,
    And joy around thee flourish!

The Fisherman.

(*From Brsseldt.*)

—o—

I

A FISHERMAN sat all day long beside a little
brook,
But all in vain ! for useless still dangled his empty
hook ;
At last it bobs ! lo ! wriggling there a tiny fish he
sees ;
Bright golden red it was in hue, and not at all at
ease.

2

" Dear fisherman ! " it thus implores with gentle
soothing speech,
" Restore me this once to the waves, I do of you
beseech ! "

"O little fish! that cannot be; 'tis useless to
   complain;
It were too great a risk for me to let you go
   again!"

3

"Yet think, kind sir, how small I am—scarce
   worth your while to cook;
I 'd ne'er be missed! Ah! then restore me once
   more to the brook!"
"Well! since thou art so delicate, and of an age
   so tender,
I 'll give you now a brief respite, and to the waves
   surrender;

4

"But when thou shalt be large and fat, be not thy
   pledge forgot!
Present thyself again to me here at this very
   spot!"
Right joyful sprang the little fish into the cooling
   flood,
And friskily swam to and fro in most ecstatic
   mood!

5

A whole year passed, the fish, grown fat and ready
    for the pot,
Himself presented faithfully just at the self-same
    spot ;
The fisherman then said, " Since thou has honestly
    behaved,
Be thou for ever free !" so thus the little fish was
    saved !

The Erl-King.

(*Goethe.*)

———o———

I

WHO rides so fast through the darkness and
    storm ?
'Tis a father supporting his child's frail form ;
He holds the boy well, with strong grasp of arm ;
He wraps him securely, he keeps him warm.

2

Father.—My son ! why hidest thou thus thy head ?
Son.—See'st thou not, father ! the Erl-king dread ?
    The dread Erl-king with his crown and train ?
Father.—My son ! *'tis the wind sweeping over the*
    plain.

3

Erl-King.—Thou charming child ! come, accom-
    pany me ;
I 'm ready to have some rare sport with thee ;

Many bright gay flowers blow on yonder
shore;
My mother's gown glitters with gold all o'er!

4

Son.—My father! my father! and dost thou not
hear
What the Erl-king is whispering in my ear?
Father.—Be calm and rest quiet, beloved child!
*'Tis the wind through the dry leaves whistling
wild!*

5

Erl-King.—Say, fairest child! wilt thou come with
me?
My lovely daughters shall wait on thee;
My daughters their nightly vigils keep,
And shall dance and sing and lull thee to
sleep!

6

Son.—My father! my father! and see'st thou not
The Erl-king's daughter on yon dark spot?
Father.—My son! my son! yes, I see quite clear;
*'Tis the old willow-tree looming grey and
drear!*

7

Erl-King.—I love thee! thy fair form doth me
  allure;
  If not willing to come, force must thee secure!
Son.—My father! my father! he fastens on me;
  The Erl-king has done me an injury!

8

The father shudders and rides on wild;
His arms encircle his sobbing child;
Arrived at his home, with trouble and dread,
Lo! there in his arms the child lay dead!

Found!

(*Goethe.*)

—o—

ONE day I sauntered in a wood to gratify my
    bent,
Having no special aim at all, nor practical intent.

Blooming beneath the shade I saw a flower of
    modest size ;
It glittered like a little star, and had two pretty
    eyes.

I wished to break it off the stem, when thus it me
    addressed :
" Why pluck me thus, to wither soon ?   Ah ! suffer
    me to rest ! "

I then, with all its tender roots, dug up the plant
    complete,
And to my garden carried it, close to my favourite
    seat ;

There, in a snug and shady spot, I planted it
  anew,
Where it expanded day by day, and still more
  lovely grew!

Barbarossa.

(*Ruckert.*)

—o—

OLD FREDERICK BARBAROSSA, styled "The
  Kaiser" in his day,
Enchanted underground survives, in castle stowed
  away;

He did not die—but still contrives himself alive to
  keep,
Concealed within those castle walls, sedately posed
  in sleep.

The splendour of his earthly court he thither with
  him bore;
And once again, in his own time, he will resume
  his power.

Upon a throne of ivory he sits with aspect grand;
And on a marble table leans, with head upon his
  hand.

His beard is not of flaxen hue, but red as fire it
    glows,
Grown through the table whereupon his head he
    doth repose.

Anon he nods, as in a dream ; his eyes half open
    blink ;
And a dwarf page, from time to time, he summons
    with a wink ;

And in his sleep he cries, "O Dwarf ! outside the
    castle hie,
And see if still around the hill the old black ravens
    fly ;

" For if still flying round about the ravens' flock
    appears,
Then must I here enchanted sleep another hundred
    years."

The Old Tobacco-Pipe.

(*A Dialogue.—Pfeffel.*)

—o—

Stranger.—Good day, old man! what hast thou
    got?
  A pipe! with rings of gold,
Formed of red clay like flower-pot!
  Pray, is it to be sold?

Old Man.—Sir! from this bowl to part were grief;
  'Twas won by a brave man
In battle from a Turkish chief
  Of some Belgradian clan.

Good booty we had there, I trow!
  Long live the Prince Eugene!
The Turkish ranks were all laid low
  Like grass upon the green!

Stranger.—Enough just now of your grand deeds,
    Old man !—and, if you 're wise,
  You 'll take this gold, whose worth exceeds
    That of the pipe you prize !

Old Man.—I 'm an old soldier, sir ! and live
    On pittance little worth;
  But this good pipe I would not give
    For all the gold on earth !

  Listen !—One day, when 'twas our lot
    To chase the foe with zest,
  A rascal janissary shot
    Our captain through the breast.

  I took him up on my grey steed,
    (He would have done it too !)
  And bore him through the fray with speed
    To a good man and true.

  I nursed him till in death he pressed
    My hand, and to me gave
  His pipe and all that he possessed ;
    Thus died my hero brave !

As for his gold, I gave the whole
  To his thrice-plundered host ;
But kept, as *souvenir*, this bowl—
  'Twas what I valued most.

Thenceforth this relic was to me
  Companion in the field ;
Both in defeat and victory
  'Twas in my boot concealed.

At Prague, amid the battle's gripe,
  A shot my right leg caught ;
My first wild thought was for my pipe ;
  My limb to me was naught !

Stranger.—Thy tale affects me, e'en to tears ;
  Who might this hero be ?
My heart his memory reveres,
  And would bewail with thee.

Old Man.—As "VALIANT WALTHER" he was
      known ;
  His home was near yon Rhine.
Stranger.—Then, 'twas my father ! and I own
  That self-same spot as mine.

Come, friend ! my house your home shall be ;
    Grim want no longer dread ;
Von Walther's wines come drink with me,
    And eat Von Walther's bread !

Old Man.—Agreed ! I 'll move when in the sky
    The morning sun shall shine ;
Thou art his heir ! so, when I die,
    Thy father's pipe be thine !

The Watchman's Call.

(*Nach Hebel.*)

—o—

[It was the custom in many German towns, some fifty years ago,
for the watchmen to proclaim each hour of night with some
suitable song or sentence.]

I

HEARKEN, good folk ! to what I tell ;
The clock strikes " TEN " upon the bell !
Now, pray and go to bed ; but yet
To put the light out don't forget ;
Soundly repose ! for Heaven doth keep
A watchful eye o'er those who sleep !

2

Hearken, good folk ! to what I tell ;
" ELEVEN" tolls on the clock bell !
To him who still is working hard,
To him who sits up playing card,
To each and all aloud I cry,
'Tis high time you to bed should hie !

3

Hearken, good folk ! to what I tell ;
'Tis MIDNIGHT ! " TWELVE " tolls on the
  bell !
Wherever, in this solemn hour,
The heart-sick soul doth grief outpour,
God grant his trouble soon may cease,
And help him now to sleep in peace !

4

Hearken, good folk ! to what I tell ;
The clock tolls " ONE " upon the bell !
Where'er, by Satan led astray,
A thief sneaks on his darksome way,—
I hope *not !* but if such there be,
Let him go home, for God doth see !

5

Hearken, good folk ! to what I tell ;
The clock strikes " TWO " upon the bell !
Whoso, by heavy care opprest,
Lies waking, still deprived of rest,
With anxious heart : Poor soul ! rely
On God's word : He 'll thy wants supply !

6

Hearken, good folk! to what I tell ;
The clock tolls " THREE " upon the bell !
The morning hovers in the sky ;
Happy if thou can'st it descry ;
Thank God ! and take fresh courage still ;
Go, work, and keep thyself from ill !

The Minstrel.

(*Goethe.*)

—o—

1

"WHAT sound is that outside I hear?
  Now o'er the bridge 'tis stealing!
Let the sweet music reach mine ear,
  Within this wide hall pealing!"
Thus speaks the King—the page runs out:
A servant comes—the King doth shout,
  "Let the old man appear!"

2

"God greet you well, each noble knight!
  God greet you, noble dames!
What heavenly stars blaze on my sight!
  Who knoweth all their names?
This hall, so full of light sublime,
Dazzles my eyes; but 'tis no time
  To revel in delight!"

3

The minstrel, closing now his sight,
  His lofty lay outpours!
Around the hall stares each bold knight,
  Each dame her fair head lowers;
Moved with the magic sounds, the King
Brings forth to him an offering,
  A chain of gold most bright!

4

"Give not to *me* this chain of gold!
  Bestow it on some knight,
With daring front the spear to hold,
  And put the foe to flight;
Thy chancellor might aptly bear,
Together with his load of care,
  This golden burden bright!

5

"I sing as sings the bird that soars
  And lodges in the tree;
The song that my own throat outpours
  Is best reward for me!
But, if I covet ought that's thine,
From golden cup the best of wine
  Let my sole payment be!"

6

'Tis by him placed ; the draught he drains :
  " Oh, sweet the cup I lift !
Oh! blest abode, where minstrel gains
  Such wine as trifling gift !
If well you fare, of me too think ;
Thank God, as I thank you, for drink
  Like this to warm the veins."

The White Stag.

(*Uhland.*)

THREE sportsmen set out with a wonderful start,
Intending to chase the famous white hart.
They laid themselves down beneath a fir-tree,
Where they had a most singular dream, all three.

First Sportsman.

"I dreamt I was beating about the bush,
When out rushed a stag with a loud *Hush ! hush !*"

Second Sportsman.

" And as from the hounds he made a spring,
I fired at his hide with a loud *Ping ! ping !*"

Third Sportsman.

" And seeing him lie on the earth all torn,
I blew a '*tarara*' upon the horn !"

.　　　.　　　.　　　.　　　.

So as they lay talking with all their might,
Out rushed the white hart before their sight;
And ere the three hunters could aim a gun,
Over hill and dale away he had run !

Hush, hush ! Ping, ping ! Tarara !

The Blind and the Lame.

(Gellert.)

—o—

A BLIND man one day chanced to meet
A lame man hobbling in the street ;
The former felt right glad to greet
One who, he hoped, might guide his feet—
"Guide thee ?" the latter says, " why, man !
Crawl by myself I scarcely can,
Whilst you can boast a famous pair
Of shoulders that my weight would bear !
Resolve at once to carry me,
And I will guide the way for thee ;
So shall thy stronger limbs be mine,
Whilst my clear eyesight shall be thine !"
Then with his crutch himself he swung,
And to the blind man's broad back clung ;
And, thus united, did these twain
Achieve what each had tried in vain !

MORAL.

Thou lack'st what some one else has got,
And dost possess what he has not;
From such defects may spring utility,
And from discrepance sociability!

The Traveller.

(*Gellert.*)

—o—

1

A TRAVELLER, by the storm dismayed,
To Jupiter devoutly prayed
    For a calm sunny day:
To move the god he tried in vain ;
The storm raged on with wind and rain,
    Impeding still his way.

2

With bitter oaths the traveller then
Accused the god of plaguing men,
    And walked on sorely troubled ;
Oft as the freshening gale repelled
His onward steps his anger swelled,
    His blasphemies were doubled !

3

At length to this ungodly scoffer
A neighbouring forest seemed to offer
    Shelter from wind and rain ;
But as he sought the friendly cover,
Afar he saw a bandit hover,
    So stood still in the rain.

4

Forthwith the bandit poised his bow,
Although relaxed by moisture now,
    And aimed with deadly art ;
But, baffled by the wind and rain,
The shaft fell harmless on the plain,
    That would have pierced his heart !

5

" O fool ! " the angry god now cries ;
" Will not this lesson make thee wise ?
    Was not the storm thy friend ?
Had I thy prayer for sunshine heard,
The arrow's course would not have erred,
    To save thee from thine end ! "

The Treasure-Diggers.

(Burger.)

—o—

A VINE-DRESSER about to die,
Collected all his children nigh,
Then said, "*Beneath our vines doth lie
A treasure.*"
            "On which spot?" they cry;
Screaming aloud;—
            "*Go dig!*" replied
The father; then, alas, he died!
Scarce had they buried the old man,
When all with might to dig began,
Plying the mattock, hoe, and spade,
Till the whole circuit they had made,
And every clod that was uplifted
Carefully through a sieve was sifted;
Then to and fro they raked the field,
Till not a small stone was concealed;

Only, *no treasure was perceived,*
And each one thought himself deceived.
But when the new year made display,
Wonder succeeded to dismay,
For every vine bore fruit threefold.
Henceforth, at last grown wise, we 're told,
They dug with vigour year by year,
Contriving still fresh gains to clear.

The Boy and the Dates.

(Pfeffel.)

——o——

A BOY was fond, as boys will be,
Of dates ; they formed his favourite dish ;
So hoping soon to rear a tree,
And thus indulge his daily wish,
He popped a date-stone in the soil.
His father, laughing, watched his toil,
And said, "Why plantest thou a date ?
My child ! thou many a year must wait ;
For know, that oft this noble tree
Full twenty years requires to grow
Ere bearing its sweet progeny ! "
Carl, scarce expecting such a blow,
Stood for awhile like one perplexed,
But soon exclaimed with cheerful face :
" To hear such news I am not vexed ;
Delay like that brings no disgrace ;
So that I may, when old, enjoy
The fruit I planted as a boy !

Æsop.

(Nicholai.)

Æsop went forth to market-town one day;
A passing traveller stopped the sage to greet,
And asked, " How long, sir, will it take me, pray,
To reach yon distant borough from this street ? "
" *Go !* " replied Æsop.   Quoth he, " Well, I know
I cannot reach the place unless I *go !*
But surely you might tell how long I 'll be ? "
Again the sage says, " *Go !* " The stranger mutters,
" This fellow is a dolt ! I plainly see
There 's nothing to be learnt from what he utters."
So off he walked.   "*Ho !*" Æsop shouts, "*one word;
Two hours will take you there.*" The stranger heard,
And stood still in amaze : " How know you now?"
Æsop retorts : " And pray, sir, tell me how
I could on such a point give my decision
Until I knew *your pace* with due precision ? "

The Ox and the Ass.

(*Pfeffel.*)

—o—

AN ox and ass, while out for walk,
Wrangle together in their talk ;
And make a wager (both have lost !)
As to which can most wisdom boast.
At last they mutually agree
The lion shall their umpire be,
And by his judgment to abide ;
Who better could the case decide ?
Both humbly bow before the throne
Whereon the beast-king sits alone ;
While he, with noble brow of scorn,
Bends on the pair an angry frown.
And thus, at length, in voice of thunder,
He roars out to their mutual wonder :
"*Fools are ye both, of basest clay !*"
Whereat they gape and sneak away.

Swiss Songs.

(*Schiller.*)

—o—

THE FISHER-BOY.

(SUNG IN THE BOAT.)

THE smiling lake how tempting seems !
On its green bank a young boy dreams ;
Celestial music greets his ear,
Like that of angels, sweet and clear ;
Waking delighted from his rest,
The waters splash against his breast ;
A voice from the deep cries : " Charming boy !
All swains like thee I would fain decoy."

THE SHEPHERD.

(SUNG ON THE MOUNTAIN.)

YE fields, farewell !
And each sunny dell !
The shepherd flies
When summer hies.

Away to the mountains! nor come ye again
Till the cuckoo's call is heard on the plain,
And the earth is clad with flowers of May,
And the streamlets flow on their winding way.

THE HUNTSMAN.

(SUNG ON THE ROCK.)

HARK! the thunder in the hills! the little bridges
    shake;
The hardy huntsman fearless doth his giddy path-
    way take;

Boldly he strides o'er fissures deep, 'mid icy fields
    of snow,
Where no spring blooms, and where no shrub was
    ever seen to grow;

While far below his feet is stretched a boundless
    sea of mist,
But not a sign of human kind, or towns where
    they exist;

Save far below between the clouds at intervals is
    seen,
Reflected in some distant lake, a field of shining
    green.

Prayer during Battle.

(*Körner.*)

—o—

1

FATHER! I call to thee!
'Mid the fumes and thunder of battle's ire,
'Mid the lightning flash of guns rattling fire,
Ruler of mortal destiny!
Father! my leader be!

2

Father! my leader be!
Lead me to victory; lead me to death!
To thy sovereign will I surrender my breath;
Lord! do what thou will'st with me;
O God! thy hand I see!

3

O God! thy hand I see,
Whether 'mid autumn's leaf-rustling glades,
Or the battle's loud roaring cannonades,
Source of grace and of clemency!
Father! oh bless thou me!

4

Father ! oh bless thou me !
Our struggle is not for the treasures of earth,
Our swords protect things of far holier worth ;
        Fall we or stand, still praised be !
        O God ! to thee I flee !

5

O God ! to thee I flee !
When the cannon shall deal its last deadly blow,
And the warm life-blood from my veins shall flow,
        I 'll flee, O my God, to thee !
        Father ! then hear thou me !

PRINTED BY BALLANTYNE AND COMPANY
EDINBURGH AND LONDON

A CLASSIFIED CATALOGUE OF HENRY S. KING & CO.'S PUBLICATIONS.

CONTENTS.

HISTORY AND BIOGRAPHY.

THE NORMAN PEOPLE, AND THEIR EXISTING DESCENDANTS IN THE BRITISH DOMINIONS AND THE UNITED STATES OF AMERICA. One handsome vol. 8vo. Price 21*s*. *[In the Press.*

This work is the result of many years of research into the history of the Norman race in England. It is generally supposed to have become extinct; but careful study has shown that it exists and forms a large part of the English people. In the course of the work the early history of the whole aristocracy is revised, reconstructed, and very many thousands of families are shown to be Norman which have never before been accounted for.

A MEMOIR OF THE LATE REVEREND DR. ROWLAND WILLIAMS, With selections from his Note-books and Correspondence. Edited by **Mrs. Rowland Williams.** With a Photographic Portrait. *[In the Press.*

THE RUSSIANS IN CENTRAL ASIA. A Critical Examination, down to the present time, of the Geography and History of Central Asia. By **Baron F. Von Hellwald,** Member of the Geographical Societies of Paris, Geneva, Vienna, &c., &c. Translated by **Lieut.-Col. Theodore Wirgman, LL.B.,** late 6th Inniskilling Dragoons; formerly of the Austrian Service; Translator into English verse of Schiller's "Wallenstein's Camp." *[Nearly ready.*

THE GOVERNMENT OF THE NATIONAL DEFENCE. From the 30th June to the 31st October, 1870. The Plain Statement of a Member. By **Mons. Jules Favre.** 1 vol. Demy 8vo. 10*s.* 6*d.*

BOKHARA : ITS HISTORY AND CONQUEST. By **Professor Arminius Vàmbèry,** of the University of Pesth, Author of "Travels in Central Asia," &c. Demy 8vo. Price 18*s.*

"We conclude with a cordial recommendation of this valuable book. In the present work his moderation, scholarship, insight, and occasionally very impressive style, have raised him to the dignity of an historian."—*Saturday Review.*

"Almost every page abounds with composition of peculiar merit, as well as with an account of some thrilling event more exciting than any to be found in an ordinary work of fiction."—*Morning Post.*

THE RELIGIOUS HISTORY OF IRELAND: PRIMITIVE, PAPAL, AND PROTESTANT; including the Evangelical Missions, Catholic Agitations, and Church Progress of the last half century. By **James Godkin,** Author of "Ireland, her Churches," &c. 1 vol. 8vo. Price 12*s.*

"For those who shun blue books, and yet desire some of the information they contain, these latter chapters on the statistics of the various religious denominations will be welcomed."—*Evening Standard.*

"Mr. Godkin writes with evident honesty, and the topic on which he writes is one about which an honest book is greatly wanted."—*Examiner.*

'ILÂM ÊN NÂS. Historical Tales and Anecdotes of the Times of the Early Khalifahs. Translated from the Arabic Originals. By **Mrs. Godfrey Clerk,** Author of "The Antipodes and Round the World." Crown 8vo. Price 7*s.*

"But there is a high tone about them, a love of justice, of truth and integrity, a sense of honour and manliness, and a simple devotion to religious duty, which however mistaken according to our lights, is deserving of every respect. The translation is the work of a lady, and a very excellent and scholar-like translation it is, clearly and pleasantly written, and illustrated and explained by copious notes, indicating considerable learning and research."—*Saturday Review.*

"Those who like stories full of the genuine colour and fragrance of the East, should by all means read Mrs. Godfrey Clerk's volume."—*Spectator.*

"As full of valuable information as it is of amusing incident."—*Evening Standard.*

ECHOES OF A FAMOUS YEAR. By **Harriet Parr,** Author of "The Life of Jeanne d'Arc," "In the Silver Age," &c. Crown 8vo. 8*s.* 6*d.*

"A graceful and touching, as well as truthful account of the Franco-Prussian War. Those who are in the habit of reading books to children will find this at once instructive and delightful."—*Public Opinion.*

"Miss Parr has the great gift of charming simplicity of style ; and if children are not interested in her book, many of their seniors will be."—*British Quarterly Review.*

HISTORY AND BIOGRAPHY—*continued.*

ALEXIS DE TOCQUEVILLE. Correspondence and Conversations with Nassau W. Senior from 1833 to 1859. Edited by **Mrs. M. C. M. Simpson.** In 2 vols., large post 8vo. 21*s.*

"Another of those interesting journals in which Mr. Senior has, as it were, crystallized the sayings of some of those many remarkable men with whom he came in contact."—*Morning Post.*

"A book replete with knowledge and thought."—*Quarterly Review.*
"An extremely interesting book."—*Saturday Review.*

JOURNALS KEPT IN FRANCE AND ITALY. From 1848 to 1852. With a Sketch of the Revolution of 1848. By the late **Nassau William Senior.** Edited by his Daughter, **M. C. M. Simpson.** In 2 vols., post 8vo. 24*s.*

"The book has a genuine historical value."—*Saturday Review.*
"The present volume gives us conversations with some of the most prominent men in the political history of France and Italy. . . Mr. Senior has the art of inspiring all men with frankness, and of persuading

them to put themselves unreservedly in his hands without fear of private circulation."—*Athenæum.*
"No better, more honest, and more readable view of the state of political society during the existence of the second Republic could well be looked for."—*Examiner.*

POLITICAL WOMEN. By **Sutherland Menzies.** 2 vols. Post 8vo Price 24*s.*

"Has all the information of history, with all the interest that attaches to biography."—*Scotsman.*
"A graceful contribution to the lighter record of history."—*English Churchman.*

"No author could have stated the case more temperately than he has done, and few could have placed before the reader so graphically the story which had to be told."—*Leeds Mercury.*

SARA COLERIDGE, MEMOIR AND LETTERS OF. Edited by her **Daughters.** 2 vols. Crown 8vo. With 2 Portraits. Price 24*s.* Second Edition, Revised and Corrected.

"We have read these two volumes with genuine gratification."—*Honr.*
"We could have wished to give specimens of her very just, subtle, and concise criticisms on authors of every sort and time—poets, moralists, historians, and philosophers. Sara Coleridge, as she is revealed, or rather reveals herself, in the correspondence, makes a brilliant addition to a brilliant family reputation."—*Saturday Review.*

"These charming volumes are attractive in two ways: first, as a memorial of a most amiable woman of high intellectual mark; and secondly, as rekindling recollections, and adding a little to our information regarding the life of Sara Coleridge's father, the poet and philosopher."—*Athenæum.*
"An acceptable record, and present an adequate image of a mind of singular beauty and no inconsiderable power."—*Examiner.*

PHANTASMION. A Fairy Romance. By **Sara Coleridge.**
[In preparation.

HISTORY AND BIOGRAPHY—*continued.*

LEONORA CHRISTINA, MEMOIRS OF, Daughter of Christian IV. of Denmark: Written during her Imprisonment in the Blue Tower of the Royal Palace at Copenhagen, 1663—1685. Translated by **F. E. Bunnett,** Translator of Grimm's "Life of Michael Angelo," &c. With an Autotype Portrait of the Princess. Medium 8vo. 12*s.* 6*d.*

"A valuable addition to history."—*Daily News.*

"This remarkable autobiography, in which we gratefully recognize a valuable addition to the tragic romance of history."—*Spectator.*

THE LATE REV. F. W. ROBERTSON, M.A., LIFE AND LETTERS OF. Edited by **Stopford Brooke, M.A.,** Chaplain in Ordinary to the Queen. In 2 vols., uniform with the Sermons. Price 7*s.* 6*d.* Library Edition, in demy 8vo, with Two Steel Portraits. 12*s.* A Popular Edition, in 1 vol. Price 6*s.*

NATHANIEL HAWTHORNE, A MEMOIR OF, with Stories now first published in this country. By **H. A. Page.** Large post 8vo. 7*s.* 6*d.*

"The Memoir is followed by a criticism of Hawthorne as a writer; and the criticism is, on the whole, very well written, and exhibits a discriminating enthusiasm for one of the most fascinating of novelists."—*Saturday Review.*

"Seldom has it been our lot to meet with a more appreciative delineation of character than this Memoir of Hawthorne."—*Morning Post.*

"He has done full justice to the fine character of the author of 'The Scarlet Letter.'"—*Standard.*

"A model of literary work of art."—*Edinburgh Courant.*

LIVES OF ENGLISH POPULAR LEADERS. No. 1.—STEPHEN LANGTON. By **C. Edmund Maurice.** Crown 8vo. 7*s.* 6*d.*

"Mr. Maurice has written a very interesting book, which may be read with equal pleasure and profit."—*Morning Post.*

"The volume contains many interesting details, including some important documents. It will amply repay those who read it, whether as a chapter of the constitutional history of England or as the life of a great Englishman."—*Spectator.*

CABINET PORTRAITS. BIOGRAPHICAL SKETCHES OF LIVING STATESMEN. By **T. Wemyss Reid.** 1 vol. crown 8vo. 7*s.* 6*d.*

"We have never met with a work which we can more unreservedly praise. The sketches are absolutely impartial."—*Athenæum.*

"We can heartily commend his work."—*Standard.*

"The 'Sketches of Statesmen' are drawn with a master hand."—*Yorkshire Post.*

VOYAGES AND TRAVEL.

ROUGH NOTES OF A VISIT TO BELGIUM, SEDAN, AND PARIS, In September, 1870—71. By **John Ashton.** Crown 8vo, bevelled boards.   Price 3*s.* 6*d.*

> This little volume derives its chief interest from the accurate descriptions of the scenes visited during the recent struggle on the Continent.

THE ALPS OF ARABIA; or, Travels through Egypt, Sinai, Arabia, and the Holy Land. By **William Charles Maughan.** 1 vol. Demy 8vo, with Map.   Price 10*s.* 6*d.*

> A volume of simple "impressions de voyage"—but written in pleasant and interesting style.

THE MISHMEE HILLS: an Account of a Journey made in an Attempt to Penetrate Tibet from Assam, to open New Routes for Commerce. By **T. T. Cooper,** author of "The Travels of a Pioneer of Commerce." Demy 8vo. Illustrated.

THE PEARL OF THE ANTILLES; THE ARTIST IN CUBA. By **Walter Goodman.**   Crown 8vo.   7*s.* 6*d.*

> "A good-sized volume, delightfully vivid, and picturesque. . . . Several chapters devoted to the characteristics of the people are exceedingly interesting and remarkable. . . . The whole book deserves the heartiest commendation . . . sparkling and amusing from beginning to end. Reading it is like rambling about with a companion who is content to loiter, observing everything, commenting upon everything, turning everything into a picture, with a cheerful flow of spirits, full of fun, but far above frivolity."—*Spectator.*
>
> "He writes very lightly and pleasantly, and brightens his pages with a good deal of humour. His experiences were varied enough, and his book contains a series of vivid and miscellaneous sketches. We can recommend his whole volume as very amusing reading."—*Pall Mall Gazette.*

FIELD AND FOREST RAMBLES OF A NATURALIST IN NEW BRUNSWICK. With Notes and Observations on the Natural History of Eastern Canada. By **A. Leith Adams, M.A.,** &c., Author of "Wanderings of a Naturalist in India," &c., &c. In 8vo, cloth. Illustrated.   14*s.*

> "Will be found interesting by those who take a pleasure either in sport or natural history."—*Athenæum.*
>
> "The descriptions are clear and full of interest, while the book is prevented from degenerating into a mere scientific catalogue by many graphic sketches of the rambles."—*John Bull.*
>
> "To the naturalist the book will be most valuable. . . . To the general reader the book will prove most interesting, for the style is pleasant and chatty, and the information given is so graphic and full, that those who care nothing for natural history as a pursuit will yet read these descriptions with great interest."—*Evening Standard.*
>
> "Both sportsmen and naturalists will find this work replete with anecdote and carefully-recorded observation, which will entertain them."—*Nature.*

TENT LIFE WITH ENGLISH GIPSIES IN NORWAY. By **Hubert Smith.**   In 8vo, cloth.   Five full-page Engravings, and 31 smaller Illustrations, with Map of the Country showing Routes.   Price 21*s.*

> "If any of our readers think of scraping an acquaintance with Norway, let them read this book. The gypsies, always an interesting study, become doubly interesting, when we are, as in these pages, introduced to them in their daily walk and conversation."—*Examiner.*
>
> "Written in a very lively style, and has throughout a smack of dry humour and satiric reflection which shows the writer to be a keen observer of men and things. We hope that many will read it and find in it the same amusement as ourselves."—*Times.*

SCIENCE.

PRINCIPLES OF MENTAL PHYSIOLOGY. With their Applications to the Training and Discipline of the Mind, and the Study of its Morbid Conditions. By **W. B. Carpenter, LL.D., M.D., F.R.S., &c.** 8vo. Illustrated.   [*Immediately.*

THE EXPANSE OF HEAVEN. A Series of Essays on the Wonders of the Firmament. By **R. A. Proctor, B.A.,** author of "Other Worlds," &c. Small Crown 8vo.   [*Shortly.*

STUDIES OF BLAST FURNACE PHENOMENA. By **M. L. Gruner,** President of the General Council of Mines of France. Translated by **L. D. B. Gordon, F.R.S.E., F.G.S., &c.** Demy 8vo. Price 7*s.* 6*d.*

These are some important practical studies by one of the most eminent metallurgical authorities of the Continent.

A LEGAL HANDBOOK FOR ARCHITECTS. By **Edward Jenkins** and **John Raymond, Esqrs.,** Barristers-at-Law. In 1 vol. Price 6*s.*

The Publishers are assured that this book will constitute an invaluable and necessary companion for every architect's and builder's table, as well as a useful introduction for architects' pupils to the practical law of their profession.

Dedicated by special permission to the Royal Institution of British Architects.

CONTEMPORARY ENGLISH PSYCHOLOGY. From the French of **Professor Th. Ribot.** An Analysis of the Views and Opinions of the following Metaphysicians, as expressed in their writings:—

James Mill, A. Bain, John Stuart Mill, George H. Lewes, Herbert Spencer, Samuel Bailey.

Large post 8vo.

PHYSIOLOGY FOR PRACTICAL USE. By various Eminent writers. Edited by **James Hinton.** 2 vols. Crown 8vo. With 50 illustrations.

These Papers have been prepared at great pains, and their endeavour is to familiarize the popular mind with those physiological truths which are needful to all who desire to keep the body in a state of health.

[*In the Press.*

THE PLACE OF THE PHYSICIAN. The Introductory Lecture at Guy's Hospital, 1873-4; to which is added

Essays on the Law of Human Life and on the Relation between Organic and Inorganic Worlds.

By **James Hinton,** Author of "Man and His Dwelling-Place." Crown 8vo. Limp cloth.

SCIENCE—*continued.*

THE HISTORY OF THE NATURAL CREATION, Being a Series of Popular Scientific Lectures on the General Theory of Progression of Species ; with a Dissertation on the Theories of Darwin and Goethe ; more especially applying them to the Origin of Man, and to other Fundamental Questions of Natural Science connected therewith. By **Professor Ernst Hæckel,** of the University of Jena. 8vo. With Woodcuts and Plates.

[In the Press.

Second Edition.

CHANGE OF AIR AND SCENE. A Physician's Hints about Doctors, Patients, Hygiène, and Society; with Notes of Excursions for health in the Pyrenees, and amongst the Watering-places of France (Inland and Sea-ward), Switzerland, Corsica, and the Mediterranean. By **Dr. Alphonse Donné.** Large post 8vo. Price 9*s.*

"A very readable and serviceable book. . . . The real value of it is to be found in the accurate and minute information given with regard to a large number of places which have gained a reputation on the continent for their mineral waters."—*Pall Mall Gazette.*

"A singularly pleasant and chatty as well as instructive book about health."—*Guardian.*

MISS YOUMANS' FIRST BOOK OF BOTANY. Designed to cultivate the observing powers of Children. From the Author's latest Stereotyped Edition. New and Enlarged Edition, with 300 Engravings. Crown 8vo. 5*s.*

"It is but rarely that a school-book appears which is at once so novel in plan, so successful in execution, and so suited to the general want, as to command universal and unqualified approbation, but such has been the case with Miss Youmans' First Book of Botany. . . . It has been everywhere welcomed as a timely and invaluable contribution to the improvement of primary education."—*Pall Mall Gazette.*

AN ARABIC AND ENGLISH DICTIONARY OF THE KORAN. By **Major J. Penrice, B.A.** 4to. Price 21*s.*

MODERN GOTHIC ARCHITECTURE. By **T. G. Jackson.** Crown 8vo. Price 5*s.*

"The reader will find some of the most important doctrines of eminent art teachers practically applied in this little book, which is well written and popular in style."—*Manchester Examiner.*

"Much clearness, force, wealth of illustration, and in style of composition, which tends to commend his views."—*Edinburgh Daily Review.*

"This thoughtful little book is worthy of the perusal of all interested in art or architecture."—*Standard.*

A TREATISE ON RELAPSING FEVER. By **R. T. Lyons,** Assistant-Surgeon, Bengal Army. Small post 8vo. 7*s.* 6*d.*

"A practical work thoroughly supported in its views by a series of remarkable cases."—*Standard.*

65, *Cornhill;* & 12, *Paternoster Row, London.*

SCIENCE—*continued.*

THE INTERNATIONAL SCIENTIFIC SERIES.

Although these Works are not specially designed for the instruction of beginners, still, as they are intended to address the *non-scientific public*, they are, as far as possible, explanatory in character, and free from technicalities ; the object of each author being to bring his subject as near as he can to the general reader.

The Volumes already Published are :—

Third Edition.

THE FORMS OF WATER IN RAIN AND RIVERS, ICE AND GLACIERS. By **J. Tyndall, LL.D., F.R.S.** With 26 Illustrations. Crown 8vo. 5*s.*

"One of Professor Tyndall's best scientific treatises."—*Standard.*

"With the clearness and brilliancy of language which have won for him his fame, he considers the subject of ice, snow, and glaciers."—*Morning Post.*

"Before starting for Switzerland next summer every one should study 'The forms of water.'"—*Globe.*

"Eloquent and instructive in an eminent degree."—*British Quarterly.*

Second Edition.

PHYSICS AND POLITICS ; OR, THOUGHTS ON THE APPLICATION OF THE PRINCIPLES OF "NATURAL SELECTION" AND "INHERITANCE" TO POLITICAL SOCIETY. By **Walter Bagehot.** Crown 8vo. 4*s.*

"On the whole we can recommend the book as well deserving to be read by thoughtful students of politics."—*Saturday Review.*

"Able and ingenious."—*Spectator.*

"A work of really original and interesting speculation."—*Guardian.*

Second Edition.

FOODS. By **Dr. Edward Smith.** Profusely Illustrated. Price 5*s.*

"A comprehensive résumé of our present chemical and physiological knowledge of the various foods, solid and liquid, which go so far to ameliorate the troubles and vexations of this anxious and wearying existence."—*Chemist and Druggist.*

"Heads of households will find it considerably to their advantage to study its contents."—*Court Express.*

"A very comprehensive book. Every page teems with information. Readable throughout."—*Church Herald.*

Second Edition.

MIND AND BODY : THE THEORIES OF THEIR RELATIONS. By **Alexander Bain, LL.D.,** Professor of Logic at the University of Aberdeen. Four Illustrations. 4*s.*

THE STUDY OF SOCIOLOGY. By **Herbert Spencer.** Crown 8vo. Price 5*s.*

ON THE CONSERVATION OF ENERGY. By **Professor Balfour Stewart.** Fourteen Engravings. Price 5*s.*

ANIMAL MECHANICS ; or, Walking, Swimming, and Flying. By **Dr. J. B. Pettigrew, M.D., F.R.S.**

LIST OF AUTHORS AND SUBJECTS OF THEIR BOOKS,

TO BE PUBLISHED IN THE

INTERNATIONAL SCIENTIFIC SERIES.

Dr. HENRY MAUDSLEY.
Responsibility in Mental Disease.

Prof. E. J. MAREY.
The Animal Frame.

{ Rev. M. J. BERKELEY, M.A., F.L.S., and M. COOKE, M.A., LL.D.
Fungi ; their Nature, Influences, and Uses.

Prof. OSCAR SCHMIDT,
(University of Strasburg).
The Theory of Descent and Darwinism.

Prof. W. KINGDOM CLIFFORD, M.A.
The First Principles of the Exact Sciences explained to the non-mathematical.

Prof. T. H. HUXLEY, LL.D., F.R.S.
Bodily Motion and Consciousness.

Dr. W. B. CARPENTER, LL.D., F.R.S.
The Physical Geography of the Sea.

Prof. WILLIAM ODLING, F.R.S.
The New Chemistry.

Prof. SHELDON AMOS.
The Science of Law.

W. LAUDER LINDSAY, M.D., F.R.S.E.
Mind in the Lower Animals.

Sir JOHN LUBBOCK, Bart., F.R.S.
The Antiquity of Man.

Prof. W. T. THISELTON DYER, B.A. B.SC.
Form and Habit in Flowering Plants.

Mr. J. N. LOCKYER, F.R.S.
Spectrum Analysis.

Prof. MICHAEL FOSTER, M.D.
Protoplasm and the Cell Theory.

Prof. W. STANLEY JEVONS.
The Logic of Statistics.

Dr. H. CHARLTON BASTIAN, M.D., F.R.S.
The Brain as an Organ of Mind.

Prof. A. C. RAMSAY, LL.D., F.R.S.
Earth Sculpture : Hills, Valleys, Mountains, Plains, Rivers, Lakes ; how they were Produced, and how they have been Destroyed.

Prof. RUDOLPH VIRCHOW,
(University of Berlin).
Morbid Physiological Action.

Prof. CLAUDE BERNARD.
Physical and Metaphysical Phenomena of Life.

Prof. A. QUETELET.
Social Physics.

Prof. H. SAINTE-CLAIRE DEVILLE.
An Introduction to General Chemistry.

Prof. WURTZ.
Atoms and the Atomic Theory.

Prof. DE QUATREFAGES.
The Negro Races.

Prof. LACAZE-DUTHIERS.
Zoology since Cuvier.

Prof. BERTHELOT.
Chemical Synthesis.

Prof. J. ROSENTHAL.
General Physiology of Muscles and Nerves.

Prof. JAMES D. DANA, M.A., LL.D.
On Cephalization ; or, Head-Characters in the Gradation and Progress of Life.

Prof. S. W. JOHNSON, M.A.
On the Nutrition of Plants.

Prof. AUSTIN FLINT, Jr. M.D.
The Nervous System and its Relation to the Bodily Functions.

Prof. W. D. WHITNEY.
Modern Linguistic Science.

Prof. BERNSTEIN (University of Halle).
Physiology of the Senses.

Prof. FERDINAND COHN,
(University of Breslau).
Thallotyphes (Algae, Lichens, Fungi).

Prof. HERMANN (University of Zurich).
Respiration.

Prof. LEUCKART (University of Leipsic).
Outlines of Animal Organization.

Prof. LIEBREICH (University of Berlin).
Outlines of Toxicology.

Prof. KUNDT (University of Strasburg).
On Sound.

Prof. LONMEL (University of Erlangen).
Optics.

Prof. REES (University of Erlangen).
On Parasitic Plants.

Prof. STEINTHAL (University of Berlin).
Outlines of the Science of Language.

Prof. VOGEL (Polytechnic Acad. of Berlin).
The Chemical Effects of Light.

ESSAYS, LECTURES, AND COLLECTED PAPERS.

IN STRANGE COMPANY; or, The Note Book of a Roving Correspondent. By **James Greenwood,** "The Amateur Casual." Crown 8vo. 6s.

MASTER-SPIRITS. By **Robert Buchanan.** Post 8vo. 10s. 6d.

"Good Books are the precious life-blood of Master-Spirits."—*Milton.*

Criticism as a Fine Art.	Birds of the Hebrides.	4. Modern Danish Ballads.
Charles Dickens.	Scandinavian Studies :—	Poets in Obscurity :—
Tennyson.	1. A Morning in Copen-	1. George Heath, the
Browning's Marteyneeo.	hagen.	Moorland Poet.
A Young English Positivist.	2. Bjornsen's Masterpiece.	2. William Miller.
Hugo in 1872.	3. Old Ballads of Den-	
Prose and Verse.	mark.	

These are some of the author's lighter and more generally interesting Essays on literary topics of permanent interest. His other prose contributions, critical and philosophical, to our literature are included in the collected editions of his works.

THEOLOGY IN THE ENGLISH POETS. Being Lectures delivered by the **Rev. Stopford A. Brooke,** Chaplain in Ordinary to Her Majesty the Queen.

MOUNTAIN, MEADOW, AND MERE; a Series of Outdoor Sketches of Sport, Scenery, Adventures, and Natural History. By **G. Christopher Davies.** With 16 Illustrations by W. HARCOURT. Crown 8vo, price 6s.

HOW TO AMUSE AND EMPLOY OUR INVALIDS. By **Harriet Power.** Fcap. 8vo. Price 2s. 6d.

What Invalids may do to Amuse Themselves.	Amusement for Invalid Children.
	To the Invalid.
What Friends and Attendants may do for them.	Comforts and Employment for the Aged.
	Employment for Sunday.
Articles for comfort in a Sick Room.	

The question, so often put by invalids, "Can you not find me something to do?" is answered at some length in this little book, which takes up a subject but little touched upon in the many manuals for nurses. [*Just out.*

STUDIES AND ROMANCES. By **H. Schutz Wilson.** 1 vol. Crown 8vo. Price 7s. 6d.

Shakespeare in Blackfriars.	Harry Ormond's Christmas Dinner.
The Loves of Goethe.	Agnes Bernauerin.
Romance of the Thames.	"Yes" or "No"?
An Exalted Horn.	A Model Romance.
Two Sprigs of Edelweiss.	The Story of Little Jenny.
Between Moor and Main.	Dining.
An Episode of the Terror.	The Record of a Vanished Life.

"Vivacious and interesting."—*Scotsman.*

"Open the book, however, at what page the reader may, he will find something to amuse and instruct, and he must be very hard to please if he finds nothing to suit him, either grave or gay, stirring or romantic, in the capital stories collected in this well-got-up volume."—*John Bull.*

ESSAYS, LECTURES, ETC.—*continued.*

SHORT LECTURES ON THE LAND LAWS. Delivered before the Working Men's College. By **T. Lean Wilkinson.** Crown 8vo, limp cloth. 2*s.*

"A very handy and intelligible epitome of the general principles of existing land laws."—*Standard.*

"A very clear and lucid statement as to the condition of the present land laws which govern our country. These Lectures possess the advantage of not being loaded with superfluous matter."—*Civil Service Gazette.*

AN ESSAY ON THE CULTURE OF THE OBSERVING POWERS OF CHILDREN, especially in connection with the Study of Botany. By **Eliza A. Youmans.** Edited, with Notes and a Supplement, by **Joseph Payne, F.C.P.,** Author of "Lectures on the Science and Art of Education," &c. Crown 8vo. 2*s.* 6*d.*

This study, according to her just notions on the subject, is to be fundamentally based on the exercise of the pupil's own powers of observation. He is to see and examine the properties of plants and flowers at first hand, not merely to be informed of what others have seen and examined."—*Pall Mall Gazette.*

THE GENIUS OF CHRISTIANITY UNVEILED. Being Essays by **William Godwin,** Author of "Political Justice," &c. Never before published. 1 vol., crown 8vo. 7*s.* 6*d.*

"Few have thought more clearly and directly than William Godwin, or expressed their reflections with more simplicity and unreserve."—*Examiner.*

"The deliberate thoughts of Godwin deserve to be put before the world for reading and consideration."—*Athenæum.*

THE PELICAN PAPERS. Reminiscences and Remains of a Dweller in the Wilderness. By **James Ashcroft Noble.** Crown 8vo. 6*s.*

"Written somewhat after the fashion of Mr. Helps's 'Friends in Council.'"—*Examiner.*

"Will well repay perusal by all thoughtful and intelligent readers."—*Liverpool Leader.*

"The 'Pelican Papers' make a very readable volume."—*Civilian.*

BRIEFS AND PAPERS. Being Sketches of the Bar and the Press. By **Two Idle Apprentices.** Crown 8vo. 7*s.* 6*d.*

"Written with spirit and knowledge, and give some curious glimpses into what the majority will regard as strange and unknown territories."—*Daily News.*

"This is one of the best books to while away an hour and cause a generous laugh that we have come across for a long time."—*John Bull.*

ESSAYS, LECTURES, ETC.—*continued.*

THE SECRET OF LONG LIFE. Dedicated by Special Permission to Lord St. Leonards. Third Edition. Large crown 8vo. 5s.

"A charming little volume."—*Times.*

"A very pleasant little book, cheerful, genial, scholarly."—*Spectator.*

"We should recommend our readers to get this book."—*British Quarterly Review.*

"Entitled to the warmest admiration."—*Pall Mall Gazette.*

SOLDIERING AND SCRIBBLING. By **Archibald Forbes**, of the *Daily News*, Author of "My Experience of the War between France and Germany." Crown 8vo. 7s. 6d.

"All who open it will be inclined to read through for the varied entertainment which it affords."—*Daily News.*

"There is a good deal of instruction to outsiders touching military life, in this volume."—*Evening Standard.*

"Thoroughly readable and worth reading."—*Scotsman.*

THE ENGLISH CONSTITUTION. By **Walter Bagehot.** A New Edition, revised and corrected, with an Introductory Dissertation on recent changes and events. Crown 8vo. 7s. 6d.

"A pleasing and clever study on the department of higher politics."—*Guardian.*

"No writer before him had set out so clearly what the efficient part of the English Constitution really is."—*Pall Mall Gazette.*

"Clear and practical."—*Globe.*

REPUBLICAN SUPERSTITIONS. Illustrated by the Political History of the United States. Including a Correspondence with M. Louis Blanc. By **Moncure D. Conway.** Crown 8vo. 5s.

"A very able exposure of the most plausible fallacies of Republicanism, by a writer of remarkable vigour and purity of style."—*Standard.*

"Mr. Conway writes with ardent sincerity. He gives us some good anecdotes, and he is occasionally almost eloquent."—*Guardian,* July 2, 1873.

STREAMS FROM HIDDEN SOURCES. By **B. Montgomerie Ranking.** Crown 8vo. 6s.

"In point of style it is well executed, and the prefatory notices are very good."—*Spectator.*

"The effect of reading the seven tales he presents to us is to make us wish for some seven more of the same kind."—*Pall Mall Gazette.*

"The tales are given throughout in the quaint version of the earliest English translators, and in the introduction to each will be found much curious information as to their origin, and the fate which they have met at the hands of later transcribers or imitators, and much tasteful appreciation of the varied sources from whence they are extracted. . . . We doubt not that Mr. Ranking's enthusiasm will communicate itself to many of his readers, and induce them in like manner to follow back these streamlets to their parent river."—*Graphic.*

MILITARY WORKS.

THE GERMAN ARTILLERY IN THE BATTLES NEAR METZ. Based on the official reports of the German Artillery. By **Captain Hoffbauer,** Instructor in the German Artillery and Engineer School. Translated by **Capt. E. O. Hollist.**

This history gives a detailed account of the movements of the German artillery in the three days' fighting to the east and west of Metz, which resulted in paralyzing the army under Marshal Bazaine, and its subsequent surrender. The action of the batteries with reference to the other arms is clearly explained, and the valuable maps show the positions taken up by the individual batteries at each stage of the contests. Tables are also supplied in the Appendix, furnishing full details as to the number of killed and wounded, expenditure of ammunition, &c. The campaign of 1870—71 having demonstrated the importance of artillery to an extent which has not previously been conceded to it, this work forms a valuable part of the literature of the campaign, and will be read with interest not only by members of the regular but also by those of the auxiliary forces.

THE OPERATIONS OF THE FIRST ARMY, UNDER STEIN-METZ. By **Von Schell.** Translated by **Captain E. O. Hollist.** Demy 8vo. Uniform with the other volumes in the Series. Price 10*s.* 6*d.*

THE OPERATIONS OF THE BAVARIAN ARMY CORPS. By **Captain Hugo Helvig.** Translated by **Captain G. S. Schwabe.** With 5 large Maps. Demy 8vo. Uniform with the other Books in the Series.

DRILL REGULATIONS OF THE AUSTRIAN CAVALRY. From an Abridged Edition compiled by CAPTAIN ILLIA WORNOVITS, of the General Staff, on the Tactical Regulations of the Austrian Army, and prefaced by a General Sketch of the Organisation, &c., of the Country. Translated by **Captain W. S. Cooke.** Crown 8vo, limp cloth.

THE OPERATIONS OF THE FIRST ARMY UNDER GEN. VON GOEBEN. By **Major Von Schell.** Translated by **Col. C. H. Von Wright.** Four Maps. Demy 8vo. 9*s.*

History of the Organisation, Equipment, and War Services of

THE REGIMENT OF BENGAL ARTILLERY. Compiled from Published Official and other Records, and various private sources, by **Major Francis W. Stubbs,** Royal (late Bengal) Artillery. Vol. I. will contain WAR SERVICES. The Second Volume will be published separately, and will contain the HISTORY OF THE ORGANISATION AND EQUIPMENT OF THE REGIMENT. In 2 vols. 8vo. With Maps and Plans. *[Preparing.*

STUDIES IN THE NEW INFANTRY TACTICS. Parts I. & II. By **Major W. Von Schereff.** Translated from the German by **Col. Lumley Graham.** Price 7s. 6d.

"Major Von Schereff's 'Studies in Tactics' is worthy of the perusal—indeed, of the thoughtful study—of every military man. The subject of the respective advantages of attack and defence, and of the methods in which each form of battle should be carried out under the fire of modern arms, is exhaustively and admirably treated ; indeed, we cannot but consider it to be decidedly superior to any work which has hitherto appeared in English upon this all-important subject."—*Standard.*

TACTICAL DEDUCTIONS FROM THE WAR OF 1870—1. By **Captain A. Von Boguslawski.** Translated by **Colonel Lumley Graham,** late 18th (Royal Irish) Regiment. Demy 8vo. Uniform with the above. Price 7s.

"Major Boguslawski's tactical deductions from the war are, that infantry still preserve their superiority over cavalry, that open order must henceforth be the main principles of all drill, and that the chassepot is the best of all small arms for precision. . . . We must, without delay, impress brain and forethought into the British Service ; and we cannot commence the good work too soon, or better, than by placing the two books ('The Operations of the German Armies' and 'Tactical Deductions') we have here criticised, in every military library, and introducing them as class-books in every tactical school."—*United Service Gazette.*

THE ARMY OF THE NORTH-GERMAN CONFEDERATION. A Brief Description of its Organisation, of the different Branches of the Service and their 'Rôle' in War, of its Mode of Fighting, &c. By a **Prussian General.** Translated from the German by **Col. Edward Newdigate.** Demy 8vo. 5s.

*** The authorship of this book was erroneously ascribed to the renowned General von Moltke, but there can be little doubt that it was written under his immediate inspiration.

THE OPERATIONS OF THE GERMAN ARMIES IN FRANCE, FROM SEDAN TO THE END OF THE WAR OF 1870—1. With Large Official Map. From the Journals of the Head-quarters Staff, by **Major Wm. Blume.** Translated by **E. M. Jones,** Major 20th Foot, late Professor of Military History, Sandhurst. Demy 8vo. Price 9s.

"The book is of absolute necessity to the military student. . . . The work is one of high merit."—*United Service Gazette.*

"The work of translation has been well done. In notes, prefaces, and introductions, much additional information has been given."—*Athenæum.*

"The work of Major von Blume in its English dress forms the most valuable addition to our stock of works upon the war that our press has put forth. Major Blume writes with a clear conciseness much wanting in many of his country's historians. Our space forbids our doing more than commending it earnestly as the most authentic and instructive narrative of the second section of the war that has yet appeared."—*Saturday Review.*

THE OPERATIONS OF THE SOUTH ARMY IN JANUARY AND FEBRUARY, 1871. Compiled from the Official War Documents of the Head-quarters of the Southern Army. By **Count Hermann Von Wartensleben,** Colonel in the Prussian General Staff. Translated by **Colonel C. H. Von Wright.** Demy 8vo, with Maps. Uniform with the above. Price 6s.

HASTY INTRENCHMENTS. By **Colonel A. Brialmont.** Translated by **Lieutenant Charles A. Empson, R.A.** Demy 8vo. Nine Plates. Price 6*s.*

"A valuable contribution to military literature."—*Athenæum.*

"In seven short chapters it gives plain directions for forming shelter-trenches, with the best method of carrying the necessary tools, and it offers practical illustrations of the use of hasty intrenchments on the field of battle."—*United Service Magazine.*

"It supplies that which our own text-books give but imperfectly, viz., hints as to how a position can best be strengthened by means . . . of such extemporised intrenchments and batteries as can be thrown up by infantry in the space of four or five hours . . . deserves to become a standard military work."—*Standard.*

"Clearly and critically written."—*Wellington Gazette.*

STUDIES IN LEADING TROOPS. By **Colonel Von Verdy Du Vernois.** An authorised and accurate Translation by **Lieutenant H. J. T. Hildyard,** 71st Foot. Parts I. and II. Demy 8vo. Price 7*s.*

*** General BEAUCHAMP WALKER says of this work:—"I recommend the first two numbers of Colonel von Verdy's 'Studies' to the attentive perusal of my brother officers. They supply a want which I have often felt during my service in this country, namely, a minuter tactical detail of the minor operations of the war than any but the most observant and fortunately-placed staff-officer is in a position to give. I have read and re-read them very carefully, I hope with profit, certainly with great interest, and believe that practice, in the sense of these 'Studies,' would be a valuable preparation for manœuvres on a more extended scale."—Berlin, June, 1872.

THE SUBSTANTIVE SENIORITY ARMY LIST, Majors and Captains. By **Captain F. B. P. White,** 1st W. I. Regiment. 8vo, sewed. 2*s.* 6*d.*

CAVALRY FIELD DUTY. By **Major-General Von Mirus.** Translated by **Captain Frank S. Russell,** 14th (King's) Hussars. Crown 8vo, limp cloth. 7*s.* 6*d.*

*** This is the text-book of instruction in the German cavalry, and comprises all the details connected with the military duties of cavalry soldiers on service. The translation is made from a new edition, which contains the modifications introduced consequent on the experiences of the late war. The great interest that students feel in all the German military methods, will, it is believed, render this book especially acceptable at the present time.

DISCIPLINE AND DRILL. Four Lectures delivered to the London Scottish Rifle Volunteers. By **Captain S. Flood Page.** A New and Cheaper Edition. Price 1*s.*

"One of the best-known and coolest-headed of the metropolitan regiments, whose adjutant moreover has lately published an admirable collection of lectures addressed by him to the men of his corps."—*Times.*

"The very useful and interesting work.—*Volunteer Service Gazette.*

INDIA AND THE EAST.

THE ORIENTAL SPORTING MAGAZINE. A Reprint of the first 5 Volumes, in 2 Volumes, demy 8vo. price 28*s*.

These volumes contain many quaint and clever papers, among which we may mention the famous Sporting Songs written by S. Y. S., of "The Boar, Saddle, Spur, and Spear," &c., &c.—Capt. MORRIS, of the Bombay Army; as well as descriptions of Hog Hunts, Fox Hunts, Lion Hunts, Tiger Hunts, and Cheeta Hunts; accounts of Shooting Excursions for Snipe, Partridges, Quail, Toucan, Ortolan, and Wild Fowl; interesting details of Pigeon Matches, Cock Fights, Horse, Tattoo, and Donkey Races; descriptions of the Origin, Regulations, and Uniforms of Hunting Clubs; Natural History of rare Wild Animals; Memoranda of Feats of Noted Horses; and Memoirs and Anecdotes of celebrated Sporting characters, &c., &c.

[Just out.

THE EUROPEAN IN INDIA. A Hand-book of Practical Information for those proceeding to, or residing in, the East Indies, relating to Outfits, Routes, Time for Departure, Indian Climate, &c. By **Edmund C. P. Hull.** With a MEDICAL GUIDE FOR ANGLO-INDIANS. Being a Compendium of Advice to Europeans in India, relating to the Preservation and Regulation of Health. By **R. S. Mair, M.D., F.R.C.S.E.,** Late Deputy Coroner of Madras. In 1 vol. Post 8vo. 6*s*.

"Full of all sorts of useful information to the English settler or traveller in India." —*Standard.*

"One of the most valuable books ever published in India—valuable for its sound information, its careful array of pertinent facts, and its sterling common sense. It is a publisher's as well as an author's 'hit,' for it supplies a want which few persons may have discovered, but which everybody will at once recognise when once the contents of the book have been mastered. The medical part of the work is invaluable."—*Calcutta Guardian.*

THE MEDICAL GUIDE FOR ANGLO-INDIANS. Being a Compendium of advice to Europeans in India, relating to the Preservation and Regulation of Health. By **R. S. Mair, F.R.C.S.E.,** late Deputy Coroner of Madras. Reprinted, with numerous additions and corrections, from "The European in India."

EASTERN EXPERIENCES. By **L. Bowring, C.S.I.,** Lord Canning's Private Secretary, and for many years the Chief Commissioner of Mysore and Coorg. In 1 vol. Demy 8vo. 16*s*. Illustrated with Maps and Diagrams.

"An admirable and exhaustive geographical, political, and industrial survey." —*Athenæum.*

"The usefulness of this compact and methodical summary of the most authentic information relating to countries whose welfare is intimately connected with our own, should obtain for Mr. Lewin Bowring's work a good place among treatises of its kind."—*Daily News.*

"Interesting even to the general reader, but more especially so to those who may have a special concern in that portion of our Indian Empire."—*Post.*

TAS-HĪL UL KALĀM; OR, HINDUSTANI MADE EASY. By **Captain W. R. M. Holroyd,** Bengal Staff Corps, Director of Public Instruction Punjab. Crown 8vo. Price 5*s*.

INDIA AND THE EAST—*continued.*

WESTERN INDIA BEFORE AND DURING THE MUTINIES.
Pictures drawn from Life. By **Major-Gen. Sir George Le Grand Jacob, K.C.S.I., C.B.** In 1 vol. Crown 8vo. 7*s.* 6*d.*

"The most important contribution to the history of Western India during the Mutinies which has yet, in a popular form been made public."—*Athenæum.*

"Few men more competent than himself to speak authoritatively concerning Indian affairs."—*Standard.*

EDUCATIONAL COURSE OF SECULAR SCHOOL BOOKS FOR INDIA. Edited by **J. S. Laurie**, of the Inner Temple, Barrister-at-Law; formerly H.M. Inspector of Schools, England; Assistant Royal Commissioner, Ireland; Special Commissioner, African Settlements; Director of Public Instruction, Ceylon.

EXTRACT FROM PROSPECTUS.

The Editor has undertaken to frame for India,—what he has been eminently successful in doing for England and her colonies, —a series of educational works, which he hopes will prove as suitable for the peculiar wants of the country as they will be consistent with the leading idea above alluded to. Like all beginnings, his present instalments are necessarily somewhat meagre and elementary; but he only awaits official and public approval to complete, within a comparatively brief period, his contemplated plan of a specific and fairly comprehensive series of works in the various leading vernaculars of the Indian continent. Meanwhile, those on his general catalogue may be found suitable, in their present form, for use in the Anglo-vernacular and English schools of India.

The following Works are now ready :—

	s. d.		*s. d.*
THE FIRST HINDUSTANI READER, stiff linen wrapper	0 6	GEOGRAPHY OF INDIA, with Maps and Historical Appendix, tracing the growth of the British Empire in Hindustan. 128 pp. Cloth.	1 6
Ditto ditto strongly bound in cloth	0 9		
THE SECOND HINDUSTANI READER, stiff linen wrapper	0 6		
Ditto ditto strongly bound in cloth	0 9		

In the Press.

ELEMENTARY GEOGRAPHY OF INDIA.

FACTS AND FEATURES OF INDIAN HISTORY, in a series of alternating Reading Lessons and Memory Exercises.

EXCHANGE TABLES OF STERLING AND INDIAN RUPEE CURRENCY, UPON A NEW AND EXTENDED SYSTEM, embracing Values from One Farthing to One Hundred Thousand Pounds, and at rates progressing, in Sixteenths of a Penny, from 1*s.* 9*d.* to 2*s.* 3*d.* per Rupee. By **Donald Fraser**, Accountant to the British Indian Steam Navigation Co., Limited. Royal 8vo. 10*s.* 6*d.*

"The calculations must have entailed great labour on the author, but the work is one which we fancy must become a standard one in all business houses which have dealings with any country where the rupee and the English pound are standard coins of currency."—*Inverness Courier.*

BOOKS FOR THE YOUNG AND FOR LENDING LIBRARIES.

LAYS OF MANY LANDS. By a **Knight Errant.** Illustrated. Crown 8vo.

Pharaoh Land.   Wonder Land.
Home Land.   Rhine Land.

SEEKING HIS FORTUNE, AND OTHER STORIES. Crown 8vo. Four Illustrations. Price 3*s.* 6*d.*

CONTENTS.—Seeking his Fortune.—Oluf and Stephanoff.—What's in a Name?—Contrast.—Onesta.

A series of instructive and interesting stories for children of both sexes, each one enforcing, indirectly, a good moral lesson.

DADDY'S PET. By **Mrs. Ellen Ross (Nelsie Brook).** Square crown 8vo, uniform with "Lost Gip." 6 Illustrations.

A pathetic story of lowly life, showing the good influence of home and of child-life upon an uncultivated but true-hearted "navvy."

THREE WORKS BY MARTHA FARQUHARSON.

Each Story is independent and complete in itself. They are published in uniform size and price, and are elegantly bound and illustrated.

I. ELSIE DINSMORE. Crown 8vo. 3*s.* 6*d.*

II. ELSIE'S GIRLHOOD. Crown 8vo. 3*s.* 6*d.*

III. ELSIE'S HOLIDAYS AT ROSELANDS. Crown 8vo. 3*s.* 6*d.*

The Stories by this author have a very high reputation in America, and of all her books these are the most popular and widely circulated. These are the only English editions sanctioned by the author, who has a direct interest in this English Edition.

LOST GIP. By **Hesba Stretton,** Author of "Little Meg," "Alone in London." Square crown 8vo. Six Illustrations. Price 1*s.* 6*d.*

*_** *A HANDSOMELY BOUND EDITION, WITH TWELVE ILLUSTRATIONS, PRICE HALF-A-CROWN.*

"Thoroughly enlists the sympathies of the reader."—*Church Review.*
"Full of tender touches."—*Noncon-*formist.
"An exquisitely touching little story."—*Church Herald.*

THE KING'S SERVANTS. By **Hesba Stretton,** Author of "Lost Gip." Square crown 8vo, uniform with "Lost Gip." 8 Illustrations. Price 1*s.* 6*d.*

Part I.—Faithful in Little. Part II.—Unfaithful. Part III.—Faithful in Much.

AT SCHOOL WITH AN OLD DRAGOON. By **Stephen J. Mac Kenna.** Crown 8vo. 5*s.* With Six Illustrations.

"At Ghuznee Villa."   In a Golden Fort.   A Baptism of Frost.
Introductory.   A Little Game.   Who Shot the Kafirs.
Henry and Amy.   True to his Salt.   John Chinaman and the
A Story of Canterbury.   Mother Moran's Enemies.   Middies.
A Disastrous Trumpet Call.   Sooka the Sycee; or, Sea
A Baptism of Fire.   Horses in Reality.

A Series of Stories of Military and Naval Adventure, related by an old Retired Officer of the Army.

FANTASTIC STORIES. Translated from the German of **Richard Leander**, by **Paulina B. Granville.** Crown 8vo. Eight full-page Illustrations.

The Magic Organ.	The Wishing Ring.	The Dreaming Beech.
The Invisible Kingdom.	The Three Princesses with	The Little Hump-Backed
The Knight who Grew	Hearts of Glass.	Maiden.
Rusty.	The Old Bachelor.	Heavenly Music.
Of the Queen who could not	Sepp's Courtship.	The Old Hair Trunk.
make Gingerbread Nuts,	Heino in the Marsh.	
and of the King who could	Unlucky Dog and Fortune's	
not play the Jew's Harp.	Favourite.	

These are translations of some of the best of Richard Leander's well-known stories for children. The illustrations to this work are of singular beauty and finish.

THE AFRICAN CRUISER. A Midshipman's Adventures on the West Coast. A Book for Boys. By **S. Whitchurch Sadler, R.N.** Three Illustrations. Crown 8vo. 3*s.* 6*d.*

A book of real adventures among slavers on the West Coast of Africa. One chief recommendation is the faithfulness of the local colouring.

THE LITTLE WONDER-HORN. By **Jean Ingelow.** A Second Series of "*Stories told to a Child.*" Fifteen Illustrations. Cloth, gilt. 3*s.* 6*d.*

" Full of fresh and vigorous fancy : it is worthy of the author of some of the best of our modern verse."—*Standard.*

" We like all the contents of the 'Little Wonder-Horn ' very much."—*Athenæum.*

" We recommend it with confidence."—*Pall Mall Gazette.*

Second Edition.

BRAVE MEN'S FOOTSTEPS. A Book of Example and Anecdote for Young People. By the Editor of " **Men who have Risen.**" With Four Illustrations. By **C. Doyle.** 3*s.* 6*d.*

" The little volume is precisely of the stamp to win the favour of those who, in choosing a gift for a boy, would consult his moral development as well as his temporary pleasure."—*Daily Telegraph.*

"A readable and instructive volume."—*Examiner.*

" No more welcome book for the schoolboy could be imagined."—*Birmingham Daily Gazette.*

Third Edition.

STORIES IN PRECIOUS STONES. By **Helen Zimmern.** With Six Illustrations. Crown 8vo. 5*s.*

"A pretty little book which fanciful young persons will appreciate, and which will remind its readers of many a legend, and many an imaginary virtue attached to the gems they are so fond of wearing."—*Post.*

"A series of pretty tales which are half fantastic, half natural, and pleasantly quaint, as befits stories intended for the young."—*Daily Telegraph.*

Second Edition.

GUTTA-PERCHA WILLIE, THE WORKING GENIUS, By **George Macdonald.** With Illustrations by **Arthur Hughes.** Crown 8vo. 3*s.* 6*d.*

" An amusing and instructive book."—*Yorkshire Post.*

" One of those charming books for which the author is so well known."—*Edinburgh Daily Review.*

"The cleverest child we know assures us she has read this story through five times. Mr. Macdonald will, we are convinced, accept that verdict upon his little work as final."—*Spectator.*

BOOKS FOR THE YOUNG, ETC.—*continued.*

THE TRAVELLING MENAGERIE. By **Charles Camden,** Author of "Hoity Toity." Illustrated by **J. Mahoney.** Crown 8vo. 3*s.* 6*d.*

"A capital little book . . . . deserves a wide circulation among our boys and girls."—*Hour.*

" A very attractive story." — *Public Opinion.*

PLUCKY FELLOWS. A Book for Boys. By **Stephen J. Mac Kenna.** With Six Illustrations. Crown 8vo. Price 3*s.* 6*d.*

" This is one of the very best 'Books for Boys' which have been issued this year."—*Morning Advertiser.*
"A thorough book for boys . . . written

throughout in a manly straightforward manner that is sure to win the hearts of the children for whom it is intended."—*London Society.*

THE GREAT DUTCH ADMIRALS. By **Jacob de Liefde.** Crown 8vo. Illustrated. Price 5*s.*

"A really good book."—*Standard.*
" May be recommended as a wholesome present for boys. They will find in it numerous tales of adventure."—*Athenæum.*

"Thoroughly interesting and inspiriting."—*Public Opinion.*
"A really excellent book."—*Spectator.*

New Edition.

THE DESERT PASTOR, JEAN JAROUSSEAU. Translated from the French of **Eugene Pelletan.** By **Colonel E. P. De L'Hoste.** In fcap. 8vo, with an Engraved Frontispiece. Price 3*s.* 6*d.*

"There is a poetical simplicity and picturesqueness; the noblest heroism; unpretentious religion; pure love, and the spectacle of a household brought up in the fear of the Lord. . . . ."—*Illustrated London News.*

"This charming specimen of Eugène Pelletan's tender grace, humour, and high-toned morality."—*Notes and Queries.*
" A touching record of the struggles in the cause of religious liberty of a real man."—*Graphic.*

THE DESERTED SHIP. A Real Story of the Atlantic. By **Cupples Howe,** Master Mariner. Illustrated by **Townley Green.** Crown 8vo. 3*s.* 6*d.*

"Curious adventures with bears, seals, and other Arctic animals, and with scarcely more human Esquimaux, form the mass of

material with which the story deals, and will much interest boys who have a spice of romance in their composition."—*Courant.*

HOITY TOITY, THE GOOD LITTLE FELLOW. By **Charles Camden.** Illustrated. Crown 8vo. 3*s.* 6*d.*

"Young folks may gather a good deal of wisdom from the story, which is written in an amusing and attractive style."—*Courant.*
"Relates very pleasantly the history of

a charming little fellow who meddles always with a kindly disposition with other people's affairs and helps them to do right. There are many shrewd lessons to be picked up in this clever little story."—*Public Opinion.*

POETRY.

LYRICS OF LOVE FROM SHAKESPEARE TO TENNYSON. Selected and arranged by **W. Davenport Adams**. Fcap. 8vo, price 3*s*. 6*d*.

> " He has the prettiest love-songs for maids."—*Shakespeare.*

DEDICATED BY PERMISSION TO THE POET LAUREATE.

WILLIAM CULLEN BRYANT'S POEMS. Red-line Edition. Handsomely bound. With Illustrations and Portrait of the Author. Price 7*s*. 6*d*.

A Cheaper Edition is also published. Price 3*s*. 6*d*.

These are the only complete English Editions sanctioned by the Author.

ENGLISH SONNETS. Collected and Arranged by **John Dennis**. Small crown 8vo. Elegantly bound, price 3*s*. 6*d*.

HOME-SONGS FOR QUIET HOURS. By the **Rev. Canon R. H. Baynes**, Editor of " English Lyrics " and " Lyra Anglicana."

Handsomely printed and bound, price 3*s*. 6*d*.

THE DISCIPLES. A New Poem. By **Harriet Eleanor Hamilton King**. Crown 8vo. 7*s*. 6*d*.

The present work was commenced at the express instance of the great Italian patriot, Mazzini, and commemorates some of his associates and fellow-workers—men who looked up to him as their master and teacher. The author enjoyed the privilege of Mazzini's friendship, and the first part of this work was on its way to him when tidings reached this country that he had passed away.

SONGS FOR MUSIC. By **Four Friends**. Square crown 8vo.

CONTAINING SONGS BY

Reginald A. Gatty.   Stephen H. Gatty.
Greville J. Chester.   J. H. E.

THE POETICAL AND PROSE WORKS OF ROBERT BUCHAANAN. Collected Edition, in 5 Vols.

Vol. I. Contains.—" Ballads and Romances ;" " Ballads and Poems of Life."
Vol. II.—" Ballads and Poems of Life ;" " Allegories and Sonnets."
Vol. III.—" Cruiskeen Sonnets ;" " Book of Orm ;" " Political Mystics."

The Contents of the remaining Volumes will be duly announced.

THOUGHTS IN VERSE. Small crown 8vo.

This is a Collection of Verses expressive of religious feeling, written from a Theistic stand-point.

COSMOS. A Poem. Small crown 8vo.
SUBJECT.—Nature in the Past and in the Present.—Man in the Past and in the Present.—The Future.

VIGNETTES IN RHYME. Collected Verses. By **Austin Dobson**. Crown 8vo. Price 5*s*.

A Collection of Vers de Société, for the most part contributed to various magazines.

NARCISSUS AND OTHER POEMS. By **E. Carpenter**. Small crown 8vo. Price 5*s*.

A TALE OF THE SEA, SONNETS, AND OTHER POEMS. By **James Howell**. Crown 8vo, cloth, 5*s*.

IMITATIONS FROM THE GERMAN OF SPITTA AND TERSTEGEN. By **Lady Durand**. Crown 8vo. 4*s*.

" An acceptable addition to the religious poetry of the day."—*Courant.*

METRICAL TRANSLATIONS FROM THE GREEK AND LATIN POETS, AND OTHER POEMS. By **R. B. Boswell**, M.A. Oxon. Crown 8vo.

POETRY—*continued.*

ON VIOL AND FLUTE. A New Volume of Poems, by Edmund W. Gosse. With a Frontispiece by W. B. Scott. Crown 8vo.

EASTERN LEGENDS AND STORIES IN ENGLISH VERSE. By Lieutenant Norton Powlett, Royal Artillery. Crown 8vo. 5s.

"Have we at length found a successor to Thomas Ingoldsby? We are almost inclined to hope so after reading 'Eastern Legends.' There is a rollicking sense of fun about the stories, joined to marvellous power of rhyming, and plenty of swing, which irresistibly reminds us of our old favourite."—*Graphic.*

EDITH; OR, LOVE AND LIFE IN CHESHIRE. By T. Ashe, Author of the "Sorrows of Hypsipyle," etc. Sewed. Price 6d.

"A really fine poem, full of tender, subtle touches of feeling."—*Manchester News.*
"Pregnant from beginning to end with the results of careful observation and imaginative power."—*Chester Chronicle.*

THE GALLERY OF PIGEONS, AND OTHER POEMS. By Theo. Marziale. Crown 8vo. 4s. 6d.

"A conceit abounding in prettiness."—*Examiner.*
"Contains as clear evidence as a book can contain that its composition was a source of keen and legitimate enjoyment. The rush of fresh, sparkling fancies is too rapid, too sustained, too abundant, not to be spontaneous."—*Academy.*

THE INN OF STRANGE MEETINGS, AND OTHER POEMS. By Mortimer Collins. Crown 8vo. 5s.

"Abounding in quiet humour, in bright fancy, in sweetness and melody of expression, and, at times, in the tenderest touches of pathos."—*Graphic.*
"Mr. Collins has an undercurrent of chivalry and romance beneath the trifling vein of good-humoured banter which is the special characteristic of his verse."—*Athenæum.*

EROS AGONISTES. By E. B. D. Crown 8vo. 3s. 6d.

"The author of these verses has written a very touching story of the human heart in the story he tells with such pathos and power, of an affection cherished so long and so secretly. . . . It is not the least merit of these pages that they are everywhere illumined with moral and religious sentiment suggested, not paraded, of the brightest, purest character."—*Standard.*

CALDERON'S DRAMAS.

THE PURGATORY OF ST. PATRICK.
THE WONDERFUL MAGICIAN.
LIFE IS A DREAM.

Translated from the Spanish. By Denis Florence MacCarthy. 10s.

These translations have never before been published. The "Purgatory of St. Patrick" is a new version, with new and elaborate historical notes.

SONGS FOR SAILORS. By Dr. W. C. Bennett. Dedicated by Special Request to H. R. H. the Duke of Edinburgh. Crown 8vo. 3s. 6d. With Steel Portrait and Illustrations.

An Edition in Illustrated paper Covers. Price 1s.

WALLED IN, AND OTHER POEMS. By the Rev. Henry J. Bulkeley. Crown 8vo. 5s.

"A remarkable book of genuine poetry."—*Evening Standard.*
"Genuine power displayed."—*Examiner.*
". . . . . . Poetical feeling is manifest here, and the diction of the poem is unimpeachable."—*Pall Mall Gazette.*
"He has successfully attempted what has seldom before been well done, viz., the treatment of subjects not in themselves poetical from a poetic point of view."—*Graphic.*
"Intensity of feeling, a rugged pathos, robustness of tone, and a downrightness of expression which does not shrink from even slang if it seem best fitted for his purpose."—*Illustrated London News.*

SONGS OF LIFE AND DEATH. By John Payne, Author of "Intaglios," "Sonnets," "The Masque of Shadows," etc. Crown 8vo. 5s.

"The art of ballad-writing has long been lost in England, and Mr. Payne may claim to be its restorer. It is a perfect delight to meet with such a ballad as 'May Margaret' in the present volume."—*Westminster Review.*

ASPROMONTE, AND OTHER POEMS. Second Edition, cloth. 4s. 6d.

"The volume is anonymous, but there is no reason for the author to be ashamed of it. The 'Poems of Italy' are evidently inspired by genuine enthusiasm in the cause espoused; and one of them, 'The Execution of Felice Orsini,' has much poetic merit, the event celebrated being told with dramatic force."—*Athenæum.*
"The verse is fluent and free."—*Spectator.*

POETRY—*continued.*

A NEW VOLUME OF SONNETS. By the **Rev. C. Tennyson Turner.** Crown 8vo. 4*s.* 6*d.*

"Mr. Turner is a genuine poet; his song is sweet and pure, beautiful in expression, and often subtle in thought."—*Pall Mall Gazette.*

"The dominant charm of all these sonnets is the pervading presence of the writer's personality, never obtruded but always impalpably diffused. The light of a devout, gentle, and kindly spirit, a delicate and graceful fancy, a keen intelligence irradiates these thoughts."—*Contemporary Review.*

GOETHE'S FAUST. A New Translation in Rime. By the **Rev. C. Kegan Paul.** Crown 8vo. 6*s.*

"His translation is the most minutely accurate that has yet been produced. . ." —*Examiner.*

"Mr. Paul evidently understands 'Faust,' and his translation is as well suited to convey its meaning to English readers as any we have yet seen."—*Edinburgh Daily Review.*

"Mr. Paul is a zealous and a faithful interpreter."—*Saturday Review.*

THE DREAM AND THE DEED, AND OTHER POEMS. By **Patrick Scott,** Author of "Footpaths between Two Worlds," etc. Fcap. 8vo, cloth, 5*s.*

"A bitter and able satire on the vice and follies of the day, literary, social, and political."—*Standard.*

"Shows real poetic power coupled with evidences of satirical energy."—*Edinburgh Daily Review.*

SONGS OF TWO WORLDS. By a New Writer. Fcap. 8vo, cloth, 5*s.* Second Edition.

"These poems will assuredly take high rank among the class to which they belong." —*British Quarterly Review, April 1st.*

"If these poems are the mere preludes of a mind growing in power and in inclination for verse, we have in them the promise of a fine poet."—*Spectator, February 17th.*

"No extracts could do justice to the exquisite tones, the felicitous phrasing and delicately wrought harmonies of some of these poems." — *Nonconformist, March 27th.*

"It has a purity and delicacy of feeling like morning air."—*Graphic, March 16th.*

THE LEGENDS OF ST. PATRICK AND OTHER POEMS. By **Aubrey de Vere.** Crown 8vo. 5*s.*

"Mr. De Vere's versification in his earlier poems is characterised by great sweetness and simplicity. He is master of his instrument, and rarely offends the ear with false notes. Poems such as these scarcely admit of quotation, for their charm is not, and ought not to be, found in isolated passages; but we can promise the patient and thoughtful reader much pleasure in the perusal of this volume." — *Pall Mall Gazette.*

"We have marked, in almost every page, excellent touches from which we know not how to select. We have but space to commend the varied structure of his verse, the carefulness of his grammar, and his excellent English." — *Saturday Review.*

FICTION.

THE OWL'S NEST IN THE CITY. In 1 vol. Cloth, crown 8vo.

TWO GIRLS. By **Frederick Wedmore,** Author of "A Snapt Gold Ring." In 2 vols. Cloth, crown 8vo.

A powerful and dramatic story of Bohemian life in Paris and in London.

JUDITH GWYNNE. By **Lisle Carr.** In 3 vols. Crown 8vo, cloth.

MR. CARINGTON. A Tale of Love and Conspiracy. By **Robert Turner Cotton.** In 3 vols. Cloth, crown 8vo.

TOO LATE. By **Mrs. Newman.** Two vols. Crown 8vo.

A dramatic love story.

LADY MORETOUN'S DAUGHTER. By **Mrs. Eiloart.** In 3 vols. Crown 8vo, cloth.

FICTION—*continued.*

HEATHERGATE. In 2 vols. Cr. 8vo, cloth. A Story of Scottish Life and Character by a new Author.

THE QUEEN'S SHILLING. By **Captain Arthur Griffiths,** Author of ". Peccavi." 2 vols.

" . . . . A very lively and agreeable novel."—*Vanity Fair.*

"'The Queen's Shilling' is a capital story, far more interesting than the meagre sketch we have given of the fortunes of the hero and heroine can suggest. Every scene, character, and incident of the book are so life-like that they seem drawn from life direct."—*Pall Mall Gazette.*

MIRANDA. A Midsummer Madness. By **Mortimer Collins.** 3 vols.

"There is not a dull page in the whole three volumes."—*Standard.*

"The work of a man who is at once a thinker and a poet."—*Hour.*

SQUIRE SILCHESTER'S WHIM. By **Mortimer Collins,** Author of "Marquis and Merchant," "The Princess Clarice," &c. Crown 8vo. 3 vols.

"We think it the best (story) Mr. Collins has yet written. Full of incident and adventure."—*Pall Mall Gazette.*

"Decidedly the best novel from the pen of Mr. Mortimer Collins that we have yet come across."—*Graphic.*

"So clever, so irritating, and so charming a story."—*Standard.*

THE PRINCESS CLARICE. A Story of 1871. By **Mortimer Collins.** 2 vols. Crown 8vo.

"Mr. Collins has produced a readable book, amusingly characteristic. . . . ."—*Athenæum.*

"Very readable and amusing. We would especially give an honourable mention to Mr. Collins's '*vers de société,*' the writing of which has almost become a lost art."—*Pall Mall Gazette.*

"A bright, fresh, and original book.'-*Standard.*

WHAT 'TIS TO LOVE. By the Author of "Flora Adair," "The Value of Fosterstown." 3 vols.

REGINALD BRAMBLE, A Cynic of the 19th Century. An Autobiography. One Volume.

"There is plenty of vivacity in Mr. Bramble's narrative."—*Athenæum.*

"Written in a lively and readable style."—*Hour.*

"The skill of the author in the delineation of the supposed chronicler, and the preservation of his natural character, is beyond praise."—*Morning Post.*

EFFIE'S GAME; HOW SHE LOST AND HOW SHE WON. By **Cecil Clayton.** 2 vols.

"Well written. The characters move, and act, and, above all, talk like human beings, and we have liked reading about them."—*Spectator.*

CHESTERLEIGH. By **Ansley Conyers.** 3 vols. Crown 8vo.

"We have gained much enjoyment from the book."—*Spectator.*

"Will suit the hosts of readers of the higher class of romantic fiction."—*Morning Advertiser.*

BRESSANT. A Romance. By **Julian Hawthorne.** 2 vols. Crown 8vo.

"The son's work we venture to say is worthy of the sire . . . The story as it stands is one of the most powerful with which we are acquainted."—*Times.*

"Pretty certain of meeting in this country a grateful and appreciative reception."—*Athenæum.*

"Mr. Julian Hawthorne is endowed with a large share of his father's peculiar genius."—*Pall Mall Gazette.*

"Enough to make us hopeful that we shall once more have reason to rejoice whenever we hear that a new work is coming out written by one who bears the honoured name of Hawthorne."—*Saturday Review.*

HONOR BLAKE: THE STORY OF A PLAIN WOMAN. By **Mrs. Keatinge,** Author of "English Homes in India," &c. 2 vols. Crown 8vo.

"One of the best novels we have met with for some time."—*Morning Post.*

"A story which must do good to all, young and old, who read it."—*Daily News.*

OFF THE SKELLIGS. By Jean Ingelow. (Her First Romance.) Crown 8vo. In 4 vols.

" Clever and sparkling."—*Standard.*

" We read each succeeding volume with increasing interest, going almost to the point of wishing there was a fifth."—*Athenæum.*

" The novel as a whole is a remarkable one, because it is uncompromisingly true to life."—*Daily News.*

SEETA. By Colonel Meadows Taylor, Author of " Tara," " Ralph Darnell," &c. Crown 8vo. 3 vols.

" The story is well told, native life is admirably described, and the petty intrigues of native rulers, and their hatred of the English, mingled with fear lest the latter should eventually prove the victors, are cleverly depicted."—*Athenæum.*

" We cannot speak too highly of Colonel Meadows Taylor's book. . . . We would recommend all novel-readers to purchase it at the earliest opportunity."—*John Bull.*

" Thoroughly interesting and enjoyable reading."—*Examiner.*

HESTER MORLEY'S PRO-MISE. By Hesba Stretton. 3 vols.

" ' Hester Morley's Promise' is much better than the average novel of the day ; it has much more claim to critical con-sideration as a piece of literary work,—not mere mechanism. The pictures of a narrow society—narrow of soul and intellect—in which the book abounds, are very clever."—*Spectator.*

" Its charm lies not so much, perhaps, in any special excellence in character, draw-ing, or construction—though all the cha-racters stand out clearly and are well sustained, and the interest of the story never flags—as in general tone and colour-ing."—*Observer.*

THE DOCTOR'S DILEMMA. By Hesba Stretton, Author of " Little Meg," &c., &c. Crown 8vo. 3 vols.

" A fascinating story which scarcely flags in interest from the first page to the last. It is all story ; every page con-tributes something to the result."—*British Quarterly Review.*

THE ROMANTIC ANNALS OF A NAVAL FAMILY. By Mrs. Arthur Traherne. Crown 8vo. 10s. 6d.

" A very readable and interesting book." —*United Service Gazette,* June 28, 1873.

" Some interesting letters are introduced, amongst others, several from the late King William IV."—*Spectator.*

" Well and pleasantly told. There are also some capital descriptions of English country life in the last century, presenting a vivid picture of England before the intro-duction of railways, and the busy life ac-companying them."—*Evening Standard.*

JOHANNES OLAF. By E. de Wille. Translated by **F. E. Bun-nett.** Crown 8vo. 3 vols.

" The art of description is fully exhibited ; perception of character and capacity for delineating it are obvious ; while there is great breadth and comprehensiveness in the plan of the story."—*Morning Post.*

THE SPINSTERS OF BLATCHINGTON. By Mar. Travers. 2 vols. Crown 8vo.

" A pretty story. Deserving of a favour-able reception."—*Graphic.*

" A book of more than average merits, worth reading."—*Examiner.*

A GOOD MATCH. By Amelia Perrier, Author of " Mea Culpa." 2 vols.

" Racy and lively."—*Athenæum.*

" As pleasant and readable a novel as we have seen this season."—*Examiner.*

" This clever and amusing novel."—*Pall Mall Gazette.*

" Agreeably written."—*Public Opinion.*

THOMASINA. By the Author of " Dorothy," " De Cressy," etc. 2 vols. Crown 8vo.

" A finished and delicate cabinet picture, no line is without its purpose, but all con-tribute to the unity of the work."—*Athe-næum.*

" For the delicacies of character-drawing, for play of incident, and for finish of style, we must refer our readers to the story itself."—*Daily News.*

" This undeniably pleasing story."—*Pall Mall Gazette.*

VANESSA. By the Author of " Thomasina." 2 vols. Crown 8vo. [*Shortly.*

FICTION—*continued.*

THE STORY OF SIR ED-WARD'S WIFE. By **Hamilton Marshall,** Author of "For Very Life." 1 vol. Crown 8vo.

"A quiet graceful little story."—*Spectator.*
"There are many clever conceits in it. . . . Mr. Hamilton Marshall can tell a story closely and pleasantly."—*Pall Mall Gazette.*

LINKED AT LAST. By **F. E. Bunnett.** 1 vol. Crown 8vo.

"'Linked at Last' contains so much of pretty description, natural incident, and delicate portraiture, that the reader who once takes it up will not be inclined to relinquish it without concluding the volume."—*Morning Post.*
"A very charming story." — *John Bull.*

PERPLEXITY. By **Sydney Mostyn.** 3 vols. Crown 8vo.

"Shows much lucidity—much power of portraiture."—*Examiner.*
"Written with very considerable power, great cleverness, and sustained interest."—*Standard.*
"The literary workmanship is good, and the story forcibly and graphically told."—*Daily News.*

MEMOIRS OF MRS. LÆTITIA BOOTHBY. By **William Clark Russell,** Author of "The Book of Authors." Crown 8vo. 7s. 6d.

"Clever and ingenious." — *Saturday Review.*
"One of the most delightful books I have read for a very long while. . . . Thoroughly entertaining from the first page to the last."—*Judy.*
"Very clever book."—*Guardian.*

CRUEL AS THE GRAVE. By the **Countess Von Bothmer.** 3 vols. Crown 8vo.

"*Jealousy is cruel as the Grave.*"
"An interesting, though somewhat tragic story."—*Athenæum.*
"An agreeable, unaffected, and eminently readable novel."—*Daily News.*

Thirty-Second Edition.
GINX'S BABY; HIS BIRTH AND OTHER MISFORTUNES. By **Edward Jenkins.** Crown 8vo. Price 2s.

Fourteenth Thousand.
LITTLE HODGE. A Christmas Country Carol. By **Edward Jenkins,** Author of "Ginx's Baby," &c. Illustrated. Crown 8vo. 5s.
A Cheap Edition in paper covers, price 1s.
"Wise and humorous, but yet most pathetic."—*Nonconformist.*
"The pathos of some of the passages is extremely touching."— *Manchester Examiner.*

Sixth Edition.
LORD BANTAM. By **Edward Jenkins,** Author of "Ginx's Baby." Crown 8vo. Price 2s.

LUCHMEE AND DILLOO. A Story of West Indian Life. By **Edward Jenkins,** Author of "Ginx's Baby," "Little Hodge," &c. Two vols. Demy 8vo. Illustrated. [*Preparing.*

HER TITLE OF HONOUR. By **Holme Lee.** Second Edition. 1 vol. Crown 8vo.
"With the interest of a pathetic story is united the value of a definite and high purpose."—*Spectator.*
"A most exquisitely written story."—*Literary Churchman.*

THE TASMANIAN LILY. By **James Bonwick.** Crown 8vo. Illustrated. Price 5s.
"The characters of the story are capitally conceived, and are full of those touches which give them a natural appearance."—*Public Opinion.*
"An interesting and useful work."—*Hour.*

MIKE HOWE, THE BUSH-RANGER OF VAN DIE-MEN'S LAND. By **James Bonwick,** Author of "The Tasmanian Lily," &c. Crown 8vo. With a Frontispiece.

FICTION—*continued.*

Second Edition.

SEPTIMIUS. A Romance. By **Nathaniel Hawthorne,** Author of "The Scarlet Letter," "Transformation," &c.   1 vol. Crown 8vo, cloth, extra gilt.   9s.

The *Athenæum* says that "the book is full of Hawthorne's most characteristic writing."

"One of the best examples of Hawthorne's writing ; every page is impressed with his peculiar view of thought, conveyed in his own familiar way."—*Post.*

PANDURANG HARI; OR, MEMOIRS OF A HINDOO. A Tale of Mahratta Life sixty years ago. With a Preface, by **Sir H. Bartle E. Frere, G.C.S.I.,** &c.   2 vols. Crown 8vo.   Price 21s.

"There is a quaintness and simplicity in the roguery of the hero that makes his life as attractive as that of Guzman d'Alfarache or Gil Blas, and so we advise our readers not to be dismayed at the length of Pandurang Hari, but to read it resolutely through. If they do this they cannot, we think, fail to be both amused and interested."—*Times.*

MADEMOISELLE JOSE-PHINE'S FRIDAYS, and other Stories. By **Miss M. Betham Edwards,** Author of "Kitty," &c.   [*Shortly.*

A collection of Miss Edwards' more important contributions to periodical literature.

Second Edition.

HERMANN AGHA. An Eastern Narrative. By **W. Gifford Palgrave,** Author of "Travels in Central Arabia," &c.   2 vols. Crown 8vo, cloth, extra gilt.   18s.

"Reads like a tale of life, with all its incidents. The young will take to it for its love portions, the older for its descriptions, some in this day for its Arab philosophy."—*Athenæum.*

"There is a positive fragrance as of newly-mown hay about it, as compared with the artificially perfumed passions which are detailed to us with such gusto by our ordinary novel-writers in their endless volumes."—*Observer.*

MARGARET AND ELIZA-BETH. A Story of the Sea. By **Katherine Saunders,** Author of "Gideon's Rock," &c. In 1 vol. Cloth, crown 8vo.

GIDEON'S ROCK, and other Stories. By **Katherine Saunders.** In one vol.   Crown 8vo.

CONTENTS.—Gideon's Rock.—Old Matthew's Puzzle.—Gentle Jack.—Uncle Ned.—The Retired Apothecary.

JOAN MERRYWEATHER, and other Stories. By **Katherine Saunders.** In one vol. Crown 8vo.

CONTENTS.—The Haunted Crust.—The Flower-Girl.—Joan Merryweather.—The Watchman's Story.—An Old Letter.

A New and Cheaper Edition, in 1 vol. each, Illustrated, price 6s., of

COL. MEADOWS TAYLOR'S INDIAN TALES is preparing for publication. The First Volume will be "The Confessions of a Thug," and will be published in December, to be followed by "Tara," "Ralph Darnell," "Tippoo Sultan."

THEOLOGICAL.

STUDIES IN MODERN PROBLEMS. A Series of Essays by various Writers. Edited by the **Rev. Orby Shipley, M.A.**

This project secures the supervision of a small number of Clergy and Laity formed of representative men in London, at both Universities, and in the Provinces, who have promised their co-operation editorially, and will act as a Committee of Reference. The first issue will consist of a series of 12 or 13 Tractates, by various writers, of 48 pages each, in a readable type, crown 8vo, at the price of 6*d.*, and will appear fortnightly for six months, by way of trial.

A Single Copy sent post free for 7*d.*
The Series of 12 Numbers sent post free for 7*s.*, or for 7*s.* 6*d.* if 13 } *if prepaid.*
Additional Copies sent at proportionate rates . . . . }

PROPOSED SUBJECTS AND AUTHORS.
(AMONGST OTHERS)

SACRAMENTAL CONFESSION.
A. H. WARD, M.A.

RETREATS FOR PERSONS LIVING IN THE WORLD.
T. T. CARTER, M.A.

ABOLITION OF THE ARTICLES.
NICHOLAS POCOCK, M.A.

CREATION AND MODERN SCIENCE.
GEORGE GREENWOOD, M.A.

MISSIONS. J. EDWARD VAUX, M.A.

CATHOLIC AND PROTESTANT.
EDWARD L. BLENKINSOPP, M.A.

SOME PRINCIPLES OF CEREMONIAL. J. E. FIELD, M.A.

THE SANCTITY OF MARRIAGE.
JOHN WALTER LEA, B.A.

RESERVATION OF THE BLESSED SACRAMENT.
HENRY HUMBLE, M.A.

CATHOLICISM AND PROGRESS.
EDMUND G. WOOD, M.A.

A LAYMAN'S VIEW OF CONFESSION.
J. DAVID CHAMBERS, M.A.

UNTIL THE DAY DAWN. Four Advent Lectures delivered in the Episcopal Chapel, Milverton, Warwickshire, on the Sunday evenings during Advent, 1870. By the **Rev. Marmaduke E. Browne.** Crown 8vo.

A SCOTCH COMMUNION SUNDAY. To which are added Certain Discourses from a University City. By **A. K. H. B.**, Author of "The Recreations of a Country Parson." Crown 8vo. Price 5*s.*

CHURCH THOUGHT AND CHURCH WORK. Edited by the **Rev. Chas. Anderson, M.A.**, Editor of "Words and Works in a London Parish." Demy 8vo. Pp. 250. 7*s.* 6*d.* Containing Articles by the Rev. J. LL. DAVIES, J. M. CAPES, HARRY JONES, BROOKE LAMBERT, A. J. ROSS, Professor CHEETHAM, the EDITOR, and others.

WORDS AND WORKS IN A LONDON PARISH. Edited by the **Rev. Charles Anderson, M.A.** Demy 8vo. 6*s.*

"It has an interest of its own for not a few minds, to whom the question 'Is the National Church worth preserving as such, and if so how best increase its vital power?' is of deep and grave importance." —*Spectator.*

EVERY DAY A PORTION: Adapted from the Bible and the Prayer Book, for the Private Devotions of those living in Widowhood. Collected and Edited by the **Lady Mary Vyner.** Square crown 8vo, printed on good paper, elegantly bound.

"Now she that is a widow indeed, and desolate, trusteth in God."

WORDS OF HOPE FROM THE PULPIT OF THE TEMPLE CHURCH. By C. J. Vaughan, D.D., Master of the Temple.

Third Edition.

THE YOUNG LIFE EQUIPPING ITSELF FOR GOD'S SERVICE. Being Four Sermons Preached before the University of Cambridge in November, 1872. By the **Rev. C. J. Vaughan, D.D.,** Master of the Temple. Crown 8vo. Price 3s. 6d.

"Has all the writer's characteristics of devotedness, purity, and high moral tone."—*London Quarterly Review.*

"As earnest, eloquent, and as liberal as everything else that he writes."—*Examiner.*

"Earnest in tone and eloquent in entreaty."—*Manchester Examiner.*

A NEW VOLUME OF ACADEMIA ESSAYS. Edited by the **Most Reverend Archbishop Manning.** Demy.

CONTENTS:—The Philosophy of Christianity.—Mystical Elements of Religion.—Controversy with the Agnostics.—A Reasoning Thought.—Darwinism brought to Book.—Mr. Mill on Liberty of the Press.—Christianity in relation to Society.—The Religious Condition of Germany.—The Philosophy of Bacon.—Catholic Laymen and Scholastic Philosophy.

WHY AM I A CHRISTIAN? By **Viscount Stratford de Redcliffe, P.C., K.G., G.C.B.** Crown 8vo. 3s. Third Edition.

"Has a peculiar interest, as exhibiting the convictions of an earnest, intelligent, and practical man."—*Contemporary Review.*

THEOLOGY AND MORALITY. Being Essays by the **Rev. J. Llewellyn Davies.** 1 vol. 8vo. Price 7s. 6d.

Essays on Questions of Belief and Practice.—The Debts of Theology to Secular Influences.—The Christian Theory of Duty.—Weak Points in Utilitarianism.—Nature and Prayer.—The Continuity of Creation.—The Beginnings of the Church.—Erastus and Excommunication.—Pauperism as produced by Wealth.—Combinations of Agricultural Labourers.—Communism.

"There is a good deal that is well worth reading."—*Church Times.*

THE RECONCILIATION OF RELIGION AND SCIENCE. Being Essays by the **Rev. T. W. Fowle, M.A.** 1 vol., 8vo. 10s. 6d.

The Divine Character of Christ.—Science and Immortality.—Morality and Immortality.—Christianity and Immortality.—Religion and Fact.—The Miracles of God.—The Miracles of Man.—A Scientific Account of Inspiration.—The Inspiration of the Jews.—The Inspiration of the Bible.—The Divinity of Christ and Modern Thought.—The Church and the Working Classes.

"A book which requires and deserves the respectful attention of all reflecting Churchmen. It is earnest, reverent, thoughtful, and courageous. . . . There is scarcely a page in the book which is not equally worthy of a thoughtful pause."—*Literary Churchman.*

HYMNS AND VERSES, Original and Translated. By the **Rev. Henry Downton.** Small crown 8vo, 3s. 6d.

"It is a rare gift and very precious, and we heartily commend this, its fruits, to the pious in all denominations."—*Church Opinion.*

"Considerable force and beauty characterise some of these verses."—*Watchman.*

"Mr. Downton's 'Hymns and Verses' are worthy of all praise."—*English Churchman.*

"Will, we do not doubt, be welcome as a permanent possession to those for whom they have been composed or to whom they have been originally addressed."—*Church Herald.*

THEOLOGICAL—*continued.*

MISSIONARY ENTERPRISE IN THE EAST. By the **Rev. Richard Collins.** Illustrated. Crown 8vo. 6s.

"A very graphic story told in lucid, simple, and modest style." — *English Churchman.*

"A readable and very interesting volume."—*Church Review.*

"It is a real pleasure to read an honest book on Missionary work, every word of which shows the writer to be a man of large heart, far-seeing views, and liberal cultivation, and such a book we have now before us."—*Mission Life.*

"We may judge from our own experience, no one who takes up this charming little volume will lay it down again till he has got to the last word."—*John Bull.*

THE ETERNAL LIFE. Being Fourteen Sermons. By the **Rev. Jas. Noble Bennie, M.A.** Crown 8vo. 6s.

"We recommend these sermons as wholesome Sunday reading."—*English Churchman.*

"Very chaste and pure in style."—*Courant.*

"The whole volume is replete with matter for thought and study."—*John Bull.*

"Mr. Bennie preaches earnestly and well."—*Literary Churchman.*

THE REALM OF TRUTH. By **Miss E. T. Carne.** Crown 8vo. 5s. 6d.

"A singularly calm, thoughtful, and philosophical inquiry into what Truth is, and what its authority."—*Leeds Mercury.*

"It tells the world what it does not like to hear, but what it cannot be told too often, that Truth is something stronger and more enduring than our little doings, and speakings, and actings." — *Literary Churchman.*

LIFE : Conferences delivered at Toulouse. Crown 8vo. 6s. By the **Rev. Père Lacordaire.**

"Let the serious reader cast his eye upon any single page in this volume, and he will find there words which will arrest his attention and give him a desire to know more of the teachings of this worthy follower of the saintly St. Dominick."—*Morning Post.*

"The book is worth studying as an evidence of the way in which an able man may be crippled by theological chains."—*Examiner.*

"The discourses are simple, natural, and unaffectedly eloquent."—*Public Opinion.*

Fourth Edition.

THOUGHTS FOR THE TIMES. By the **Rev. H. R. Haweis, M.A.,** "Author of Music and Morals," etc. Crown 8vo. 7s. 6d.

"Bears marks of much originality of thought and individuality of expression."—*Pall Mall Gazette.*

"Mr. Haweis writes not only fearlessly, but with remarkable freshness and vigour. In all that he says we perceive a transparent honesty and singleness of purpose."—*Saturday Review.*

SPEECH IN SEASON. A New Volume of Sermons. By the **Rev. H. R. Haweis.** [*Preparing.*

Second Edition.

CATHOLICISM AND THE VATICAN. With a Narrative of the Old Catholic Congress at Munich. By **J. Lowry Whittle, A.M.,** Trin. Coll., Dublin. Crown 8vo. 4s. 6d.

"We may cordially recommend his book to all who wish to follow the course of the Old Catholic movement." — *Saturday Review.*

THEOLOGICAL.—*continued.*

Second Edition.

SCRIPTURE LANDS IN CONNECTION WITH THEIR HISTORY. By **G. S. Drew, M.A.**, Vicar of Trinity, Lambeth, Author of "Reasons of Faith." Bevelled boards, 8vo. Price 10*s.* 6*d.*

"Mr. Drew has invented a new method of illustrating Scripture history — from observation of the countries. Instead of narrating his travels, and referring from time to time to the facts of sacred history belonging to the different countries, he writes an outline history of the Hebrew nation from Abraham downwards, with special reference to the various points in which the geography illustrates the history. . . He is very successful in picturing to his readers the scenes before his own mind."—*Saturday Review.*

Second Edition.

NAZARETH: ITS LIFE AND LESSONS. By the **Rev. G. S. Drew**, Vicar of Trinity, Lambeth. Second Edition. In small 8vo, cloth. 5*s.*

"A singularly reverent and beautiful book."—*Daily Telegraph.*
"Perhaps one of the most remarkable books recently issued in the whole range of English theology."—*Churchman's Magazine.*

THE DIVINE KINGDOM ON EARTH AS IT IS IN HEAVEN. By the **Rev. G. S. Drew**, Author of "Nazareth: its Life and Lessons." In demy 8vo, bound in cloth. Price 10*s.* 6*d.*

"Thoughtful and eloquent. . . . Full of original thinking admirably expressed."—*British Quarterly Review.*
"Entirely valuable and satisfactory. . . . . . There is no living divine to whom the authorship would not be a credit."—*Literary Churchman.*

SIX PRIVY COUNCIL JUDGMENTS — 1850-1872. Annotated by **W. G. Brooke, M.A.**, Barrister-at-Law. Crown 8vo. 9*s.*

THE MOST COMPLETE HYMN BOOK PUBLISHED.

HYMNS FOR THE CHURCH AND HOME. Selected and Edited by the **Rev. W. Fleming Stevenson**, Author of "Praying and Working."

The Hymn-book consists of Three Parts:—I. For Public Worship.—II. For Family and Private Worship.—III. For Children: and contains Biographical Notices of nearly 300 Hymn-writers, with Notes upon their Hymns.

* * *Published in various forms and prices, the latter ranging from* 8*d. to* 6*s. Lists and full particulars will be furnished on application to the Publisher.*

WORKS OF THE LATE REV. F. W. ROBERTSON.

NEW AND CHEAPER EDITIONS.

SERMONS.

Vol.	I. Small crown 8vo.	Price 3*s.* 6*d.*
,,	II. Small crown 8vo.	Price 3*s.* 6*d.*
,,	III. Small crown 8vo.	Price 3*s.* 6*d.*
,,	IV. Small crown 8vo.	Price 3*s.* 6*d.*

EXPOSITORY LECTURES ON ST. PAUL'S EPISTLE TO THE CORINTHIANS. Small crown 8vo. 5*s.*

AN ANALYSIS OF MR. TENNYSON'S "IN MEMORIAM." (Dedicated by permission to the Poet-Laureate.) Fcap. 8vo. 2*s.*

THE EDUCATION OF THE HUMAN RACE. Translated from the German of **Gotthold Ephraim Lessing.** Fcap. 8vo. 2*s.* 6*d.*

LECTURES AND ADDRESSES, WITH OTHER LITERARY REMAINS. By the late **Rev. Fredk. W. Robertson.** A New Edition, including a Correspondence with Lady Byron. With Introduction by the **Rev. Stopford A. Brooke, M.A.** In One Vol. Uniform with the Sermons. Price 5*s.*   [*Preparing.*

A LECTURE ON FRED. W. ROBERTSON, M.A. By the **Rev. F. A. Noble,** delivered before the Young Men's Christian Association of Pittsburgh, U.S. 1*s.* 6*d.*

WORKS BY THE REV. STOPFORD A. BROOKE, M.A.

Chaplain in Ordinary to Her Majesty the Queen.

THE LATE REV. F. W. ROBERTSON, M.A., LIFE AND LETTERS OF. Edited by **Stopford Brooke, M A.**, Chaplain in Ordinary to the Queen.

In 2 vols., uniform with the Sermons. Price 7*s.* 6*d.*

Library Edition, in demy 8vo, with Two Steel Portraits. 12*s.*
A Popular Edition, in 1 vol. Price 6*s.*

THEOLOGY IN THE ENGLISH POETS. Being Lectures delivered by the **Rev. Stopford A. Brooke,** Chaplain in Ordinary to Her Majesty the Queen.

Third Edition.

CHRIST IN MODERN LIFE. Sermons Preached in St. James's Chapel, York Street, London. Crown 8vo. 7*s.* 6*d.*

"Nobly fearless and singularly strong. . . . carries our admiration throughout."—*British Quarterly Review.*

Second Edition,

FREEDOM IN THE CHURCH OF ENGLAND. Six Sermons suggested by the Voysey Judgment. In 1 vol. Crown 8vo, cloth. 3*s.* 6*d.*

"A very fair statement of the views in respect to freedom of thought held by the liberal party in the Church of England."—*Blackwood's Magazine.*

"Interesting and readable, and characterised by great clearness of thought, frankness of statement, and moderation of tone."—*Church Opinion.*

Seventh Edition.

SERMONS Preached in St. James's Chapel, York Street, London. Crown 8vo. 6*s.*

"No one who reads these sermons will wonder that Mr. Brooke is a great power in London, that his chapel is thronged, and his followers large and enthusiastic.

They are fiery, energetic, impetuous sermons, rich with the treasures of a cultivated imagination."—*Guardian.*

THE LIFE AND WORK OF FREDERICK DENISON MAURICE: A Memorial Sermon. Crown 8vo, sewed. 1*s.*

THE CORNHILL LIBRARY OF FICTION.

3s. 6d. per Volume.

IT is intended in this Series to produce books of such merit that readers will care to preserve them on their shelves. They are well printed on good paper, handsomely bound, with a Frontispiece, and are sold at the moderate price of **3**s. **6**d. each.

FOR LACK OF GOLD. By **Charles Gibbon**.

GOD'S PROVIDENCE HOUSE. By **Mrs. G. L. Banks**.

ROBIN GRAY. By **Charles Gibbon**. With a Frontispiece by **Hennessy**.

KITTY. By **Miss M. Betham-Edwards**.

READY MONEY MORTIBOY. A Matter-of-Fact Story.

HIRELL. By **John Saunders**. Author of "Abel Drake's Wife."

ONE OF TWO. By **J. Hain Friswell**, Author of "The Gentle Life," etc.

ABEL DRAKE'S WIFE. By **John Saunders**.

THE HOUSE OF RABY. By **Mrs. G. Hooper**.

A FIGHT FOR LIFE. By **Moy Thomas**.

OTHER STANDARD NOVELS TO FOLLOW.

65, *Cornhill ; and* 12, *Paternoster Row, London.*